The Case of the Klutzy King Charles

A Thousand Islands Doggy Inn Mystery

B.R. Snow

Copyright © 2017 B.R. Snow
ISBN: 978-1-942691-35-8

Website: www.brsnow.net/
Twitter: @BernSnow
Facebook: facebook.com/bernsnow

Cover Design: Reggie Cullen
Cover Photo: James R. Miller

Other Books by B.R. Snow

The Thousand Islands Doggy Inn Mysteries

- The Case of the Abandoned Aussie
- The Case of the Brokenhearted Bulldog
- The Case of the Caged Cockers
- The Case of the Dapper Dandie Dinmont
- The Case of the Eccentric Elkhound
- The Case of the Faithful Frenchie
- The Case of the Graceful Goldens
- The Case of the Hurricane Hounds
- The Case of the Itinerant Ibizan
- The Case of the Jaded Jack Russell

The Whiskey Run Chronicles

- Episode 1 – The Dry Season Approaches
- Episode 2 – Friends and Enemies
- Episode 3 – Let the Games Begin
- Episode 4 – Enter the Revenuer
- Episode 5 – A Changing Landscape
- Episode 6 – Entrepreneurial Spirits
- Episode 7 – All Hands On Deck
- The Whiskey Run Chronicles – The Complete Volume 1

The Damaged Posse

- American Midnight
- Larrikin Gene
- Sneaker World
- Summerman
- The Duplicates

Other Books

- Divorce Hotel
- Either Ore

To the Cullen Family

We'll always miss the ones we lose, and we will never forget.

Chapter 1

In my dream, I'm being chased.

And although I'm desperate to get away and find sanctuary, my unseen pursuer is rapidly gaining ground. I hear footsteps on both sides of me and a soft whine - no make that a whimper - and I want to look back over my shoulder, but I'm afraid to even open my eyes much less turn for fear of what I might find lurking, tracking me down, relentlessly closing the gap between us. I continue my slow stroll forward on the soft, wet sand in total darkness.

Apparently in my dreams, just like in daily life, I avoid strenuous physical activity like it was the plague.

I feel the creature's wet, cold touch. On my left arm, my feet, now my neck, and I squeeze my eyes tight as if believing what I can't see can't hurt me. Suddenly, a heavy weight drops on my chest, and it's clear that I've lost my chance to escape. Faced with the choice between surrender or fighting for my life, I decide I need a moment to consider the implications of both options. To help clear my thoughts I reach for a bite-sized and slowly chew the delicious morsel of nougat topped with caramel and peanuts wrapped in chocolate, and I smile. But as the weight on my chest begins to impact my breathing, I realize this is not the time for grins and snickers.

I laugh silently at what I consider a witty pun and unwrap a second one-bite wonder.

But my laughter and snack are cut short when the weight on my chest deepens, and I feel sharp points pressing against my ribcage. I take a deep breath and wait for the thrust of the honed edge that's certain to come my way and destroy several internal organs I really need in good working condition. Then I feel a rough, wet object slowly making its way across my neck. Up and down my sunburned skin it goes, and I'm horrified about what is next to come. I struggle, but my arms are pinned, and I'm unable to respond and fend off the attack. I consider screaming, but before I can make a sound, I hear the sound of two loud splashes. Have my attacker and I somehow fallen into some unseen body of water? I anticipate a drenching, but apart from my wet neck that my attacker appears to have a special fondness for, the rest of me is dry as a bone.

Then it begins to rain, and I'm soaked by the sudden torrent. The rush of water pulls me out of my deep sleep, and I open my eyes. I blink several times and glance around my surroundings, baffled.

Chloe is stretched out across my chest with her front paws pressed firmly against my ribs and giving Al and Dente the stink eye for having woken her. The two Goldens on either side of my recliner are staring at me and apparently refreshed by their swim. The wag of their tails reminds me of a metronome set to an up-tempo, four-four time, Captain gives my neck one final lick then decides the idea of an early morning dip sounds good. He lumbers to the edge of the pool, jumps in as if it's second nature, and is soon churning laps.

I slide Chloe off my chest and sit up to pet the Goldens that won't take no for an answer and watch Captain swim back and forth. The early morning sun is slowly working its way above the horizon behind me, and it's already apparent that the day will be hot and dry. At least it will be as soon as the two gallons of water Al and Dente shook all over me dries.

"Merry Christmas!" Josie and Chef Claire say in unison as they exit the house through the sliding glass doors that lead out to the covered patio area next to the pool.

"Wow. That's right," I say, smiling over my shoulder at them. "I almost forgot. Merry Christmas."

Josie hands me a mug of coffee, and I take a sip. They both stretch out in recliners on either side of me and accept the affections of Al and Dente while trying to protect their morning coffee.

"I can't believe I was out here all night." I yawn and attempt a stretch that is cut short by Chloe's hostile takeover of the recliner. "Chloe, why don't you join Captain for a swim?"

Chloe opens one eye, considers the idea, then dozes off.

"You need to speak her language," Josie says, laughing as she reaches for a tennis ball next to her recliner. "Chloe, hey, girl." She bounces the tennis ball on the tile a few times until she has the Aussie's attention. Then she fires it in the pool. Chloe tears after the ball and launches herself into the water and is soon tussling with Captain for control.

"Great idea," Chef Claire says as she grabs three more tennis balls and throws them into the deep end. Both Goldens are soon back in the pool with the other two dogs, and we sit back to enjoy our morning wake up call.

"You were out last night," Josie says, taking a sip. "We tried to wake you, then decided you looked pretty comfortable."

"I had a dream," I say, trying to remember some of the details.

"Was it any good?" Josie says.

"Something was chasing me, and I was trying to escape."

"You were running?"

"No, I think it was more of a leisurely stroll."

Josie and Chef Claire both laugh. We continue to watch the dogs frolicking in the pool.

"Well, they sure wouldn't be doing that at home today," Josie says.

"No, they wouldn't," I say with a shake of my head. "But it seems a bit odd to be on the beach on Christmas Day, doesn't it?"

"I'm fine with it," Chef Claire says with a chuckle.

"I just checked the weather in Clay Bay."

"How bad is it?"

"Twenty degrees, six inches of snow, but it's supposed to warm up later, and there's a fifty-fifty chance of freezing rain this afternoon."

"Yuk." I scowl at the mental picture of a miserable winter day then laugh when Captain places a paw on Chloe's head and playfully dunks her as she grabs for one of the tennis balls. "It's almost like he can walk on water. He's so comfortable in there."

"Yeah, it must be the webbed feet," Josie says staring out at the Newfie who was continuing to dominate the pool. "He's amazing in the water."

"So, what's the schedule for the day?" Chef Claire says, finishing her coffee.

"We have to be at my mom's place by nine for breakfast," I say, sliding my empty coffee mug under the recliner. "Her traditional Mimosas and Eggs Benedict."

"Now there's a Christmas tradition I can get behind," Chef Claire says as she yawns and stretches her arms over her head.

"After that, we'll open presents. Then she's having her annual Christmas barbecue for all her friends. I don't know what you guys will want to do after that, but I'm pretty sure I'll need a long nap."

"We'll have to leave the dogs in her garage until they dry off and we get a brush through them," Josie says. "I can't believe how much sand those guys collect in a day."

"Yeah, tell me about it," Chef Claire says, staring at her Goldens. "And I've got two of them to deal with."

"But you wouldn't change a thing, right?" Josie says.

"Not a chance," Chef Claire says, climbing out of her recliner and heading to the edge of the pool.

Al and Dente notice her standing there, swim over for a quick hello, then make a beeline for Captain who is trying to hog all four tennis balls. The Newfie somehow manages to secure all of them in his mouth then climbs out of the pool. He heads our way, and before we can get to safety, he drops the balls at our feet and shakes vigorously.

"Geez, Captain," Josie says, wiping her face with the back of her sleeve. "You goofball."

Captain takes this as an invitation and drapes his front paws over Josie's shoulders. She momentarily disappears from view as the massive dog shows her how much he adores her. She gently pushes him away, laughing the entire time.

"They definitely need to dry off in the garage," I say, laughing as I wipe myself off.

"Yeah, your mom may be a converted dog lover, but I doubt she'd enjoy having to deal with that while she's trying to make breakfast."

"No, I'm sure she wouldn't. But if I can catch her standing by the pool later, who knows?" I say, laughing at the prospect.

"You're just still steamed because she made fun of what you were wearing last night," Chef Claire says. "What was that thing anyway?"

"It was a Christmas blouse," I say, immediately on the defensive. "Hibiscus and Poinsettia."

"More like a Christmas tent," Josie says with a frown. "And so much green and red."

"Hey, it's festive. And comfortable. I am supposed to be on vacation, right?" I sit up in the recliner. "If we can't figure out a way to get the dogs to shake all over her, maybe I can just *accidentally* bump her into the pool."

"Ho, ho, ho. Nice Christmas spirit," Josie says, gently punching me on the shoulder.

"Hey, even Santa would laugh at that."

Chapter 2

I showered, changed into a pair of linen shorts and a solid color lavender blouse I knew would pass muster with my mother, and sat down in the great room that overlooked the patio and pool. I glanced around the house, a multi-level, seven-bedroom structure with more interesting nooks and crannies than the English muffin I'd eaten earlier. My mother bought the place last year for what she considered a song: A song with a whole lot of trailing zeros as I reminded her on a regular basis.

She maintains she purchased it as an investment, which I'm sure is partially true, but her primary motive was to find a place where the three of us could stay when we visited. Getting me down here during the winter had been one of her goals for years since she hated the fact that we didn't see each other for up to three months at a time. I'd resisted for several years, citing my work responsibilities at the Inn as an excuse, but Sammy and Jill, our two most-trusted staff members, had proven more than capable of running the place in our absence. Over time, my mother wore me down, and now I'm forced to admit that I love the idea of spending my winters in sand and sun instead of snow and ice and bone-chilling cold. Now I'm spending my winters waking up every morning to a cool ocean breeze and a view of the water that, although different, rivals the one we enjoy back home.

Outside, the dogs were still swimming and roughhousing, and I was sure they'd be more than ready for an extended nap by the time we got to my mom's house located a quarter-mile away down the beach. I stretched my legs out then wiggled my toes and felt the early morning breeze drift through the house. I picked up a tinge of salt in the air and was about to close my eyes and drift off when Chef Claire came out of her bedroom working an earring into one ear as she approached. She sat down across from me and gave my outfit a nod of approval. She slid the other earring into place then gently shook her head at me, causing the earrings to sway back and forth and sparkle in the early morning light.

"What do you think?"

"Very nice. Are those the ones my mom got you for your birthday?"

"Yeah, I love them, but I'm nervous about wearing them when I'm working."

"Because you're worried they'll end up in somebody's soup, right?"

"Just my luck, one of them would fall into Josie's food," Chef Claire said.

"You've seen her eat. I doubt if she'd even notice."

We were both still laughing when Josie walked into the great room. She glanced back and forth at us and frowned.

"What did I miss?"

"We were just discussing your amazing ability to focus on the task at hand and ignore distractions," I said.

"Yeah, I bet," Josie said, twirling the pair of sandals she was holding. "You guys ready to go?"

"We are," I said, standing up and heading for the sliding glass doors.

We paused before stepping out onto the patio.

"How are we going to do this?" I said.

"I was just thinking the same thing," Chef Claire said. "I really don't feel like getting drenched again."

"Watch and learn," Josie said, stepping out onto the patio and whistling once sharply.

The dogs stopped roughhousing, climbed out of the pool, and made a beeline for her. She whistled again, and the dogs stopped and stared at her with their heads cocked.

"Stay," Josie commanded. "Shake. No, stay. Shake."

All four dogs vigorously shook, and a cascade of water emerged from their fur and fell harmlessly onto the patio.

"Good dogs," Josie said, glancing over her shoulder at us. "Who's the good dogs?"

"Showoff," Chef Claire said, stepping outside onto the patio to greet Al and Dente.

We did our best to stay dry as we rubbed the dogs' heads and then headed for the gate that sat in the middle of the perimeter fence surrounding the property. With the dogs leading the way, we made our way down to the beach and headed toward the water's edge. The stiff onshore wind had dropped overnight, and the gentle breeze that remained felt great against my face as the water licked my feet. The dogs did a decent job of staying out of the ocean as they trotted down the flat stretch of sand near the water. Chloe appeared to be playing tag with the Goldens, and all three were growling playfully at each other. Then I stopped when I noticed Captain sitting on his haunches staring out at the ocean. I nudged Josie and nodded my head at the Newfie.

"What is it, Captain?" Josie said, approaching the dog who maintained his intense stare.

The dog woofed loudly and looked back at Josie.

"Do you see something out there?" she said, holding a hand up to block the glare.

Captain barked several times in rapid succession, then sprung forward into the water and began churning his way out to sea.

"Captain!" Josie shouted. "Get back here!"

"Where the heck is he going?" I said, concerned but still admiring the dog's power.

"I have no idea," Josie said, uncertain about her next move. "What on earth did he see?"

I stared out and caught a glimpse of what appeared to be a yellow object barely floating about a hundred yards from the beach. I thought I saw movement next to the object but couldn't be sure. Captain continued his beeline toward it, his focus complete.

"If I'm not mistaken," Chef Claire said, "I'd swear that's an arm holding onto a submerged kayak."

I glanced out at blue water tipped with white from the chop and got a better look at the yellow object that was coming in and out of view.

"I think you're right," I said, squinting hard as I knelt down to rub Chloe's head. She was on her haunches next to me and also staring out at the water.

"What the heck are we going to do?" Josie said, hands on hips. She began pacing back and forth on the sand, her eyes never leaving the Newfie.

"I think we're just going to have to wait and see," I said. "And hope Captain knows what he's doing."

"Well, he's certainly a much better swimmer than we are. Look at him go," Chef Claire said, holding Al and Dente by their collars. Neither dog appeared ready to follow Captain, but she wasn't taking any chances.

Captain came to a stop and began swimming in small circles as if sizing up the situation. We continued to stare out at the water, and I placed my hand on Josie's shoulder in an effort to allay her fears. She jumped back when I touched her, startled.

"I'm sorry," I said. "What do you want to do?"

"If he doesn't head back this way soon, I'm going in after him," she said, glancing around. "I knew we should have gotten a kayak."

"Try to relax," I said. "He seems to be doing just fine."

Then my phone buzzed, and I checked the number and answered.

"Hey, Mom," I said, distracted.

"Well, Merry Christmas to you, too, darling."

"I'm sorry, Mom, but we're dealing with a bit of a situation here."

I briefly explained what was happening and then I glanced down the beach and caught a glimpse of her standing on her front porch waving to me.

"I'll call you right back," I said, hanging up and giving her a quick wave.

Captain was now slowly making his way back toward shore. We continued to stare out at the water, trying to figure out exactly what was happening and what had caused the dog to swim out into open water. The Newfie continued to powerfully chug his way through the water, and it soon became apparent that he had something in his mouth, as well as something hanging onto his back. Moments later, my mouth dropped when I finally saw the person floating on her back as Captain slowly dragged her through the water, pulling her along by the arm. But I was completely bewildered when I saw the small dog perched precariously on Captain's back. The Newfie's focus was unshakeable, and he spotted Josie on the shore and made a beeline for her. As he got closer, Josie and I waded into the water, followed closely by Chloe, and we swam toward the Newfie. When we reached Captain, Josie grabbed the unconscious woman's arms and gently pulled her toward shore. I lifted the small dog off Captain's back and held it tight to my chest. It was trembling with fear, and it nestled its head under my shoulder as I waded back to shore.

Chef Claire helped Josie with the woman, and they gently stretched her out on the sand. She was definitely still alive, but her breathing was shallow and labored. I set the small dog down on the sand, and it shook vigorously. Only then did I recognize the breed. The Cavalier King Charles spaniel was still trembling with fear, but slowly finding its footing. Chloe and the Goldens approached and tentatively said hello, and the King Charles, too tired or frightened to play or run away, sat down in the sand and let the other dogs give him the once-over.

I reached for my phone, then shook my head when I realized I'd just taken it for a lengthy swim.

"Chef Claire, can you please call my mom and have her call for an ambulance?"

"You ruin your phone?" Josie said, not glancing up from the unconscious woman she was giving CPR.

"Yeah."

"Me too, I'm sure," she said, focused on the woman stretched out on the sand.

I took my first good look at her. She was somewhere in her thirties, wearing a tee-shirt over her swimsuit, and had an irregular tan. Tourist, I decided. Captain approached and stared at her. I reached down to stroke the dog's head, but he ignored me and continued to focus on the woman, obviously concerned about her well-being. Josie continued administering CPR, and the woman slowly began to regain consciousness. She coughed, turned her head to one side and vomited salt water. Then she closed her eyes again.

"Your mom said the ambulance is on the way," Chef Claire said. "And she's bringing towels and water."

"Thanks," I said, glancing down the beach and seeing my mother hustling her way across the sand. I had to give her credit. She's was making a lot better time than I would have despite the load she was carrying. She slowed to a walk when she got close and tossed both Josie and I a towel. Josie gently wiped the woman's face then accepted a bottle of water from my mother. Josie and my mother helped her sit up in the sand and held the bottle close to her mouth. She took a sip, then greedily sucked on the bottle for more.

"Easy," Josie said. "Not too much at once."

"The poor thing," my mother said, staring at her.

"Do you know her, Mom?"

"No, I don't think I do," she said, shaking her head. "Is that a Cavalier King Charles?"

"It is," I said, picking the spaniel up and wrapping the still trembling dog in one of the towels. "He's terrified, but I think he's okay."

We heard the sound of an ambulance off in the distance that was getting louder by the moment.

"They'll be here soon," my mother said, then glanced at the Newfie. "Captain saw them and just swam out and rescued them?"

"Yes, he certainly did," I said, shaking my head in disbelief.

"How on earth did he know how to do that?" my mother said, frowning.

"Instinct, I imagine," I said, shrugging. "It was pretty amazing."

Captain continued to watch the woman closely. She was very groggy and drifting in and out of consciousness. The dog nuzzled the side of her neck, and she opened her eyes.

"Is that my hero?" the woman said before drifting off again.

Captain focused on the dog I was holding. I lowered the dog and Captain sniffed then nuzzled the King Charles. The small dog wiggled in my arms, and I gently set him down on the sand. He seemed to prance after he found his footing, trotted about ten feet across the sand, then tripped over a piece of driftwood and fell flat on his face in the soft sand.

"I think he might be a bit of a klutz," my mother said, bending down to help the dog onto his feet.

"He's probably just a bit disoriented," I said.

The King Charles shook the sand off, then trotted off in the other direction. Seconds later, the dog had managed to get one of his front paws stuck in a conch shell and was hopping on three legs as he tried to free himself. My mother bent down, gently removed the shell from the dog's paw, and petted the King Charles. The dog tolerated the attention for a moment, then trotted off again and managed to trip over the same piece of driftwood as before.

"Poor little guy. We better get him up to the house before he hurts himself," my mother said, doing her best not to laugh. "Do you need me to stay until the ambulance arrives?"

"No, I think we're good, Mom. If you can take care of the dog, that would be great. He's probably dehydrated so get some water in him. I'd wait a bit before you give him anything to eat, but see how he responds and play it by ear."

"Got it. I'll be waiting at the house," she said, scooping up the dog and wrapping it in the towel. "Take all the time you need."

I watched her head down the beach back toward her house then focused on the woman in the sand who continued to drift in and out of consciousness. Josie continued to slowly give her water. All four dogs watched the action closely. Two paramedics appeared at the edge of the sand carrying a stretcher and what appeared to be a portable oxygen tank. They broke into a run and headed straight for us.

"Okay, hang in there," Josie said to the woman. "Help is here, and they're going to get you to the hospital."

"Dr-drink," the woman said.

Josie gave her another sip, then sat back in the sand as the paramedics approached.

"O," the woman whispered.

"O?" Josie said, frowning. "What are you trying to say?"

"O," the woman said, blinking rapidly before her eyes closed and stayed shut. "O-wen."

"Owen?" Josie said, glancing up at me. "Who the heck is Owen?"

Chapter 3

We stayed with the unknown woman until the paramedics had finished their work. They wrapped her in a blanket, covered her mouth and nose with an oxygen mask then carried her across the sand, strapped to a stretcher. We waited until we heard the sound of the ambulance driving away then walked down the beach to my mother's house. We put the dogs in the garage and headed inside through a door that led directly into the kitchen. My mother was on the floor playing with the freshly-bathed King Charles. When we entered, my mother climbed to her feet and gave each of us a hug.

"Merry Christmas, darling," she said, squeezing the air out of me.

"Merry Christmas, Mom," I said, grimacing. "How's the little guy doing?"

"Apart from him constantly bumping into everything in sight, I think he's fine. I gave him a bath, which he loved, then he had a little snack. He's a cute little bugger."

"He is indeed," I said, nodding as I studied the chestnut and white dog with big, round, dark brown eyes that made me melt. He cocked his head at me and wagged his tail. "No collar or tag on him. I guess we'll need to hang onto him until his owner gets out of the hospital. Or maybe she has family down here who could take him."

Josie sat down on the floor and patted the tile with her palms. The King Charles padded across the floor toward her, then bumped into one of the legs on the kitchen table. Looking more embarrassed than hurt, the dog shook his head then continued across the floor ending up in Josie's arms.

"Klutzy is one thing, but that's not normal," I said, sitting down on the floor next to Josie.

"No, it's not," Josie said, holding the dog with both hands out in front of her. "His left pupil is almost fully dilated. In this light, I'd expect both of them to be pretty small."

"Anisocoria?" I said, frowning. "Is that the right term?"

"Well done, Snoopmeister," Josie said, laughing. "Somebody's finally been doing her homework."

"I've been working my way through the book alphabetically," I said, shrugging.

"What is it?" my mother said, sliding across the tile to get a closer look at the King Charles.

"One of his pupils is markedly larger than the other," Josie said, gently brushing the dog's fur away from his eyes and pointing. "See it?"

"Yes," my mother said, closely studying the dog's eyes. "What causes it?"

"Sometimes it's just there from birth and not a problem. But it can also indicate a lot of things," Josie said, setting the dog down. "Nerve disease, glaucoma, cancer. This guy can't be more than a couple of years old, so I doubt if it's anything you'd expect to see in an older dog. Given where we found him, I'm going to guess it was caused by some sort of trauma that happened to him while he was in that kayak."

"But anisocoria wouldn't necessarily be the cause of his clumsiness, right? That wouldn't cause him to bump into tables."

"You are on fire today," Josie said. "Well done. You're right, it wouldn't necessarily cause him to do that."

"Thanks," I said, beaming.

Truth be told, I have been doing a little late-night reading in some of Josie's veterinary textbooks. I have been learning a few things, but primarily they serve as a cure for insomnia.

"Okay, Dr. Doolittle," she said. "You want to continue with the diagnosis?"

"Well," I said, gently stroking the dog's head. "If it was brought on by trauma, he might have a concussion. And if the little guy got hit in the head, I'd also be willing to guess that he might have a detached retina. That could explain why he's having a hard time navigating."

"I'm impressed," Josie said, nodding. Then she caught the look I was giving her. "I'm not joking. Really. That's exactly what I'm thinking."

"Wow. How about that?" I said, grinning. "So, what do we do?"

"Well, I'm not qualified to work on eyes," Josie said. "At least when it comes to doing eye surgery."

"What are you talking about?" I said, frowning. "I've watched you perform brain surgery."

"Yeah, but eyes are different," she said, shaking her head. "They're tricky. And I never focused on them in school. It's very specialized work."

"And brain surgery is like cutting a sandwich?" I said.

"You know what I mean," she said, gently punching me on the shoulder.

"You think he might need surgery?" my mother said.

"It's possible," Josie said. "Do you know if there's a vet ophthalmologist on Grand Cayman?"

"I'm not sure," she said, reaching for her phone. "But if there is, Dr. Wallace will know."

"Who's he?" I said.

"Oh, he's a wonderful man. He's been a vet down here forever," she said, typing a search term into her phone and waiting for the results to return. She scrolled down then nodded. "What do you know? Dr. Wallace is certified in ophthalmology."

"That's good news," Josie said, climbing to her feet. "I don't think we need to bother him on Christmas Day. The little guy seems okay, but we should keep a close eye on him and not let him play with the bruisers. Even a love tap from Captain could do some more damage if he's concussed."

"We can put him in my bedroom," my mother said as she scooped the dog up in her arms.

"We'll try to get hold of this Dr. Wallace tomorrow," Josie said.

"There's no need to do that, dear," my mother said, gently stroking the King Charles' head. "You'll meet him this afternoon."

"He's coming to your barbecue?" I said, also stroking the dog's head.

"Darling, everybody comes to my Christmas barbecue," she said as she headed out of the kitchen carrying the dog. Then she stopped and turned around. "Oh, why don't the two of you grab a change of clothes from the closet and put yours in the dryer. And after you sweep up all the sand on my kitchen floor, maybe take another shower. You both look like a couple of drowned rats. After you're presentable, we'll open presents."

She shook her head at us and headed off down the hall.

"There's the mother I know," I said, shaking my head. "I was starting to worry."

"She's really taking this dog-lover thing seriously," Josie said. "Did you see the way she was looking at the King Charles?"

"Yeah, I was starting to feel bad about what I said this morning," I said. "And then she made that crack about looking like a drowned rat."

"So?"

"So, now I think I definitely want to push her in the pool," I said, laughing.

We changed clothes, tossed our wet ones in the dryer, then headed to the garage where Chef Claire was already brushing Al and Dente. She glanced up when we entered and shook her head in disbelief.

"Feel like building a sandcastle?" she said, nodding at the pile near her feet.

I knelt down to pet Chloe who was giving me a head-cocked stare. She was almost dry and had an expectant look on her face.

"What?" I said to her.

Chloe headed for the shelves that ran along one side of the garage and hopped up on her back legs. She grabbed a dog brush in her mouth, trotted back to me, and dropped it at my feet. Then she sat down and waited for me to pick it up. I surrendered and started to gently brush her.

"It's their world," Josie said, laughing. "We only live in it." She stretched out on the floor and pulled Captain close. She gave him a long hug, he responded by climbing on top of her and pinning her shoulders to the garage floor. She struggled to get out from under him, then sat up. Captain draped himself across her lap, and she vigorously rubbed his head.

"How did you know what to do?" Josie said to the Newfie. The dog thumped his tail and snorted contentedly. "Where did that come from?"

"It was pretty amazing," Chef Claire said, tossing the dog brush aside. Al and Dente nuzzled each other briefly then stretched out on the floor. "Where do those instincts come from?"

"Beats me," Josie said, giving Captain a gentle thump on the back. "He saved both their lives. You think we should go visit her in the hospital?"

"Good idea," I said, nodding. "Maybe we can fit it in tomorrow. But I have no idea when."

Tomorrow was going to be packed with activity. Josie and I had to visit the new animal clinic we were opening to do a final walkthrough before we opened the doors on New Year's Day. And in the afternoon, we were meeting Chef Claire at our new restaurant that was about to open. Based on what we'd been told, everything was ready to go at both places, but until we had a chance to confirm it with our own eyes, I remained cautiously optimistic. Adding the task of getting the King Charles to the vet, locating someone responsible for the spaniel, not to mention checking in on the woman Captain had pulled out of the water, made for a very full day. But as I was quick to remind myself on a regular basis, other people would kill to have the same list of things to worry about as I did.

Like the King Charles and a variety of other animals walking around with nowhere to go, I could be surrounded by strangers without the companionship of friends or family. Especially on Christmas Day.

Or like the woman Captain had saved from certain death, I could be flat on my back in the hospital, alone and scared, wondering where I was and how I'd gotten there.

I glanced over at Captain, a very special creature who had ventured out into dangerous ocean waters to rescue a complete stranger and her dog without giving a thought to his own well-being. Now, instead of prancing around and narcissistically calling attention to himself for a job well done, he was sound asleep in Josie's lap, snoring softly without a care in the world.

I, along with everyone else, could learn a lot from that dog.

Chapter 4

Given that the morning had gotten away from us, we jointly decided to wait to open presents until later that evening after the barbecue had ended. As soon as that decision was made, the three of us pitched in to help my mother and Henry, the man who maintained the property and lived in the guesthouse, get ready for the party. My mother put us in charge of decorating the lawn and pool area, most of which consisted of stringing lights, streamers, and two dozen Chinese lanterns she wanted surrounding the sitting area on the lawn.

By the time we had finished, the smells coming from the grill and smoker were torturing us, and the sun was high and beating down on us. We opted for a dog-free swim in the pool, then headed inside to shower and get dressed. By the time we made it back outside, several guests had already arrived and were lounging on the lawn, sipping cocktails. The setting was casual, as most social events in the islands were, and it would have been easy to mistake the guests as a collection of regular folks enjoying a relaxing afternoon with some friends. But as I looked around the lawn, I recognized several people I knew were heavy hitters with a lot of financial and political clout.

Of particular interest to me was Gerald, the Finance Minister, who was a business associate and close personal friend of my mother. We had a somewhat rocky relationship based on a situation that had occurred during our previous visit. I considered his somewhat loose interpretation of the rules about mixing personal business with the responsibilities of a government minister disturbing, while he considered those rules merely *suggested guidelines* as opposed to hard and fast caveats. They were, as he liked to remind me, just something that came with the job and needed to be carefully managed to ensure that the economy continued to move forward. Part of the cost of doing business, Gerald liked to say, and an important part of the development process. Although, when pressed, he would concede a highly profitable one.

But despite his tendency to bend the rules in his and his business associates favor, as well as line his own pockets in the process, on a personal level, I liked the guy a lot. He had a permanent smile and a booming laugh and seemed to be the sort of person who, if you were in trouble, would give you the shirt off his back. And then, as my mother was quick to point out, take back two of yours in the process.

Gerald was talking to another man, and they were sipping what I assumed to be Mudslides, a popular drink I'd developed a fondness for. The other man, gray-haired and distinguished, had to be in his late sixties, and he was smiling in my direction as Gerald pointed me out from across the lawn. Then he waved me over, and I walked toward him enjoying the feel of the soft, cool grass against my bare feet.

"Hello, Gerald," I said, going in for a hug and a kiss on the cheek. "Merry Christmas."

"Merry Christmas, Suzy," he boomed. "It's so good to see you. I guess I need to stay on my toes now that you're down here, right?"

"I've found I only need to stay on my toes when I'm in it up to my neck, Gerald," I said, giving him a coy smile.

"Didn't I tell you she was a firecracker?" Gerald said to the other man. "Suzy, I'd like to introduce you to Dr. Oliver Couch."

"Dr. Couch?" I said, smiling at him. "Let me guess, psychiatrist, right?"

Although I was pretty sure he'd heard the joke a hundred times, he laughed long and hard.

"Most clever," he said. "It's so nice to meet you. Gerald has told me many wonderful things about you. And Merry Christmas."

"Same to you," I said. "What sort of doctor are you?"

"These days I spend most of my time as a general physician, but I do find myself in surgery from time to time. Mostly hearts."

"You're a heart surgeon?" I said, impressed.

"He's a magician when it comes to hearts," Gerald said. "And if mine ever starts giving me trouble, he's the guy I want working on it."

"He's just being kind," Dr. Couch said, glancing at the Finance Minister. "But treating Gerald's heart problems might be a bit tricky because it would take forever to find it."

"Oh, so it's going to be one of those days, is it?" Gerald said, laughing. "In addition to his other duties, Oliver is also the Chief Medical Officer at the hospital just down the road."

"Really?" I said, my neurons firing. "You wouldn't know the status of a woman who was brought in earlier today, would you?"

"Do you mean the young woman who was rescued from the water by a dog?" he said, raising an eyebrow at me.

"That's the one."

"As a matter of fact, I do," he said. "I heard the call for an ambulance come in, and since I was close by at the time, I headed straight to the hospital. We're very light-staffed on holidays, so I thought I might be able to help."

"And?"

"She's fine," he said, smiling. "She was severely dehydrated, but after a couple of hours on an IV, she perked right up. We rechecked her vitals, scolded her severely for doing something as stupid as getting lost overnight on the water in a kayak, then sent her on her way."

"That's great," I said. "I'm glad to hear she's...did you just say you sent her on her way? As in discharged?"

"Yes," Dr. Couch said, nodding. "About two hours ago." He noticed the odd look I was giving him. "What?"

"It just seems odd. When we saw her on the beach, she looked like she was at death's door."

"That was the dehydration," he said. "But as I said, as soon as we got fluids in her, she perked right up. All her vitals were perfect when we let her go. If they hadn't been, she'd still be there."

"Yes, I'm sure," I said, frowning. "Did she happen to mention her dog?"

"Her dog?" Dr. Couch said. "No, I don't believe she did. At least, not to me."

"That's odd. Did she say where she was going?"

"All she said was that she needed to get out of the hospital as soon as possible since it was Christmas Day, and she had somewhere to go. And because it is Christmas, we did everything we could to make sure she didn't spend it alone in the hospital."

"Did she mention who she was going to visit? You know, a family member. Maybe a husband or boyfriend?"

"Again, I don't believe she did," Dr. Couch said. "Excuse me for asking, but why all the questions?"

"Force of habit, primarily," I said, shrugging.

Gerald laughed. Dr. Couch frowned and glanced back and forth at us confused.

"Suzy has a reputation for being a bit...I'm gonna go with *inquisitive.*"

I made a face at Gerald, then focused on the doctor.

"I'm asking because we have her dog."

"I see," Dr. Couch said. "I'm surprised she didn't mention it."

"Yeah, me too," I said.

"Well, I'm sure she'll show up at some point looking for it," Gerald said. "I need a refill. Can I bring you another, Oliver? Suzy?"

"Yes, thanks so much, Gerald," Dr. Couch said, handing him his empty glass.

"No, I'm good, thanks," I said, still frowning.

If it had been me, one of the first things I would do after regaining consciousness would be to ask about where my dog was and how it was doing. And I was very surprised that the woman had been released from the hospital so soon after being admitted with a serious case of dehydration. But I reminded myself that I was in the Cayman Islands and that things ran differently down here than they did back at home. And perhaps the hospitals weren't as worried about generating revenue or possibly getting sued than those in the States. I was pretty steamed about the prospect that the woman could have taken off without even trying to find out where her dog was. But given the ordeal she'd been through, I decided to lighten up a bit and reserve judgment for a few days until she'd had some time to fully recover and retrace her steps. Eventually, I finally decided, she would show up looking for the King Charles.

"Are you okay?" Dr. Couch said softly as he studied my face.

"Me? I'm fine. Why do you ask?"

"You just seemed to drift off for a few moments," he said.

"Oh, that," I said, waving it off. "Don't worry about that. I do it all the time."

"Interesting."

"Not really."

"Okay," he said, laughing and shaking his head. "So, tell me about this dog that saved that woman's life."

"We were walking along the beach, Captain spotted them, then just swam out and brought them back in to shore. It was incredible to watch."

"Is the dog around?"

"I'm sure he's here somewhere," I said, looking around the lawn. "There he is."

Captain was off by himself on his back, rolling on the grass with all four paws in the air. He was snorting with delight, then he hopped to his feet and sneezed loud enough to be heard across the lawn.

"A Newfoundland, right?" Dr. Couch said, admiring the massive dog.

"Yes, he certainly is. Gorgeous, huh?"

"He's magnificent. But he must be hot in that fur coat."

"Well, we keep a close eye on all the dogs when it comes to the heat. They only get to go to the beach in the morning or around sunset. The rest of the time they're at home with the pool and air conditioning."

"I see," Dr. Couch said, nodding. "So, he's adjusting well to life down here?"

"Well, based on what we watched him do this morning, I'd have to say he's off to a good start."

Chapter 5

"Hey, Mom. What's that thing sitting on the edge of the pool?" I said from the comfort of my recliner.

"Nice try, darling," my mother said, shaking her head at me. "You're off your game tonight. You'll have to do much better than that."

"Did you tell her?" I said, glancing over at Josie.

"Not me," she said, dribbling ice cream all over her blouse. "Dang it." She sat up and dabbed at the stain with her napkin. "I almost made it through a meal without spilling."

"Chef Claire?" I said, glancing over at her. She was carefully picking a chicken breast apart to make sure it was free of bones and feeding small pieces to all four dogs that were giving her their undivided attention.

"I didn't say a word," she said, rubbing Dente's head as the dog gently took a piece of chicken out of her hand.

"I overheard you, darling," my mother said, sitting down at the table next to Chef Claire. "Throwing your mother in the pool on Christmas? Ho, ho, ho. You should be ashamed of yourself."

"Told you," Josie said, laughing.

"You deserved it, Mom," I said, ignoring Josie. "Some of those cracks about what I was wearing last night were uncalled for."

"Oh, you mean that *delightful* Christmas-camping ensemble you had on? I think I saw Larry the Cable Guy modeling it in the Dick's Sporting Goods fall catalog."

Josie and Chef Claire laughed way too long, and I scowled at them. But I let it go and focused on my bowl of ice cream. My mother grabbed a chicken breast and began pulling it apart. The number of hovering dogs increased to six as my mom's two basset-bloodhound mixes, Summer and Winter, inched closer to the action.

"Great party, Mrs. C.," Chef Claire said, feeding Captain a piece of chicken.

"Thanks, dear," my mother said. "And as soon as the last of the guests hit the road, we'll open presents."

"It's pretty late, Mom," I said, setting my empty bowl aside. "We can do it in the morning if you want to wait."

"Not open presents on Christmas Day?" she said, frowning. "It doesn't seem right."

"It's fine by me," Josie said.

"Me too," Chef Claire chimed in.

"Yeah, let's wait," I said. "It'll be like having two Christmases."

"Okay," my mother said, shrugging. Then she glanced across the lawn at a couple and two young girls who were sitting by themselves at a table chatting and laughing. "Did you guys know about those two?"

All three of us shook our heads as we studied the couple.

"No," I said, smiling as I stared across the lawn. "I almost fell over earlier when I realized what was going on."

"Me too," Josie said.

"Good for them," Chef Claire said. "I think they make a cute couple."

Rocco, our head bartender from C's in Clay Bay who had volunteered to come to Grand Cayman to help us get the new restaurant ready for its grand opening, slipped his arm over the shoulder of the woman sitting next to him. She rested her head against him and smiled contentedly. Teresa Williams, the woman who was running our new animal shelter, laughed at something one of her daughters said and nudged Rocco with her elbow.

"Well, Teresa sure doesn't have to worry about feeling safe," Chef Claire said, laughing.

Josie and I, along with my mother, laughed along. Rocco, a man with a past that included several years working the dark side of the street for a crime boss, was not someone to be trifled with. And despite the thousands of people who came to eat and drink at C's each year, we rarely had a problem with unruly patrons. And when we did, Rocco had a gift for making sure it didn't last long. Now completely reformed and leading the straight life, Rocco had become an integral member of our extended family and did a great job as our bar manager. But as I watched him interact with Teresa and her daughters, I realized that he had changed again. Instead of merely being happy, he seemed totally content, at peace with himself and the world that surrounded him. To be honest, as happy as I was for both of them, I had to admit feeling a touch of envy.

"Look at him," Josie said as if reading my mind. "He's a goner."

"Yeah," I said, grinning without taking my eyes off them. "And she's right there with him."

"I thought I noticed something the last time I was down here," Chef Claire said. "But I didn't want to say anything until I was sure."

Chef Claire had made a couple of trips during the summer and fall to check on the progress of the new restaurant. Things hadn't been moving at a pace we liked, but as soon as Rocco arrived, work began to get done on time, and the construction crew we had hired developed what Rocco called...my mind went blank. I glanced over at Chef Claire who was feeding the last of the chicken to the dogs.

"What's the expression Rocco uses to describe a strong work ethic?"

"A *lavish focus* on the task at hand," Chef Claire said.

"That's a nice way of saying, 'Get it done if you don't want your thumbs broken.' He wouldn't have to tell me twice," Josie said, laughing.

"Shhhh," I said, grinning. "Here they come."

The two young girls led the way and sprinted across the lawn then dropped to the grass near the pool as the dogs greeted them. Soon they were rolling around on the lawn laughing as they fought off all six. Captain placed a paw on one of the girls' chest, pinning her to the ground as he licked her face. She squealed with delight and tried to roll away. Al and Dente, their tails wagging furiously, were draped across the other girl and she almost disappeared from view.

"Hey, Rocco, Teresa," I said, nodding at the pile of dogs surrounding the two girls. "Sorry about that."

"Don't worry about it," Teresa said, holding Rocco's hand. "They love it."

"Camila, Dalila?" my mother said to the two girls. "I think Santa left some presents here for you. They're in a bag under the tree if you'd like to go grab it."

The two girls, nine and ten and spitting images of their mother, climbed out from underneath the dogs and made a beeline across the lawn toward the house.

"You didn't need to do that," Teresa said, shaking her head at my mother.

"You let us worry about what we need to do, dear," my mother said, gently placing a hand on her arm. "Oh, how I envy you." My mother shot me a quick glance to make sure I was paying attention. "Those two girls are incredible. What I wouldn't give…"

"Please, don't start, Mom," I said, shaking my head.

"Now you know what you can give your mom next Christmas," Josie said.

"Yeah, that would definitely beat a pair of socks," Chef Claire said, grinning at me.

I scowled at them then turned to Rocco, desperate for a new topic of conversation. "What time do you need us there tomorrow?"

"Well, they're finishing up the painting in the morning," Rocco said. "Feel free to stop by after one if that works for you."

I glanced at Josie and Chef Claire. Josie nodded. Chef Claire shrugged.

"I'll be there by eight," Chef Claire said. "So whenever you finish up with Teresa, just stop by."

"I can't wait for you to see the shelter," Teresa said. "I still can't believe it."

We'd met Teresa during our last trip when we'd been looking for the owners of some lost dogs we'd found on the beach during a major storm. My mother's dogs were actually siblings from the litter of puppies we'd rescued, and the puppies' parents, a male bloodhound and female basset hound, were now permanent residents at the Doggy Inn back home. At the time, Teresa had been trying to operate an animal shelter out of her home, and the storm had pretty much destroyed the property. Shortly after that, we'd asked Teresa to run the new animal shelter we were having built near our new restaurant. As far as new businesses went, and as our accountant had been very quick to remind us, the shelter, from a financial perspective, would undoubtedly be a loser with a capital L. But since making any money from it was way down our list of priorities, we'd set it up as a non-profit and my mother had put the squeeze on several of her local friends for donations. And since Josie and I had no plans to take a salary, the place would be able to sustain itself for the foreseeable future.

Teresa, previously teetering on the edge financially, would finally be able to relax and take care of her daughters without fear of bankruptcy, and a whole bunch of animals would have a place to live and get the medical care they required. We knew that our new business venture would never rival that of a Wall Street leveraged buyout or hostile takeover, but I'd put the smiles on our faces up against any of the Greed Heads when it came to job satisfaction and personal fulfillment.

But I digress.

Camila and Dalila came out of the house, each of them holding one handle of the large bag my mother had placed all their gifts in. The dogs approached, sniffed the bag, and trailed at their heels as they struggled to make their way across the lawn.

"Hey, girls," Rocco called out. "Why don't you just leave the bag there and we'll grab it when we head to the car?"

The two girls looked at each other, decided Rocco's suggestion made a lot of sense, then set the bag down on the grass and dashed toward us.

"You guys ready to go home?" Teresa said, hugging both girls when they arrived.

"Can we open presents tonight?" Camila said, glancing at her sister for support.

Teresa glanced at Rocco who smiled and shrugged.

"Sure. Why not?" Teresa said. "What do you have to say to Mrs. C. and the girls?"

Both girls approached us individually, offered their thanks, and gave us warm hugs. Then they said their goodbyes to all the dogs.

"Thanks, again," Teresa said. "We'll see you in the morning. You ready to go, Rock?"

"I'm ready," Rocco said, standing up. "Thanks so much. This was great. Merry Christmas."

"Same to you, *Rock*," I said, grinning at the nickname.

"As in, he's my rock," Teresa said, squeezing his hand.

"Got it," I said, nodding. "See you guys tomorrow."

We watched them head across the lawn toward their car. Rocco grabbed the bag of gifts, seemed surprised by the weight and glanced back at my mother with a shake of his head at her generosity, then put the bag in the trunk. They drove off, and we all sat back to enjoy the sudden quiet. A gentle breeze had kicked up and carried the scent of a wide variety of plants and flowers that surrounded the property. I closed my eyes and let my senses run wild.

Even if this place wasn't actually paradise, I'd be willing to bet I could see it from here.

A few minutes later I opened my eyes when I heard my mother collecting the plastic bowls and spoons we'd used for the ice cream. She stacked them up in her arms and then began heading for the house. She seemed to miss a step, stumbled forward, then dropped the bowls. They bounced off the tile work surrounding the pool, and she scooped down to pick them up. Without thinking, I hopped up from my recliner.

"Let me help you, Mom," I said, bending down to grab one of the bowls.

"Why thank you, darling," my mother said, taking a step to one side to give me room.

As I brushed past her, she gave me a hip-check, and before I knew what hit me, I was suspended in mid-air, then fell into the pool with a loud splash. The dogs took it as an invitation for a late-night swim and jumped in to join me. Soon, I was splashing and trying to fend off six dogs who all wanted to play and were vying for my attention. I stood up in the shallow end and brushed my soaked hair away from my face as I glared at her.

"You're really not funny, Mom."

"Disagree," all three of them said in unison, roaring with laughter.

Chapter 6

We ushered all four dogs outside to the patio and turned on the overhead misting system we'd had installed that lowered the external temperature by almost twenty degrees. We filled several water bowls, made sure there was an ample supply of dog toys nearby, double-checked to make sure all the gates were secured, and then said goodbye to them.

"Okay, guys," Josie said, opening the patio door. "Try to stay out of trouble."

"Do you think they have any idea how good they've got it?" I said, laughing as I followed her back inside.

"You bet they do," she said. "You don't see any of them trying to get away, do you?"

We headed for the garage and hopped into the jeep my mother had lent us. I waited for the garage door to open then backed out and headed down the driveway that was surrounded on both sides by multicolored bougainvillea. We made our way through the traffic that was light and dominated by tourists in rental vehicles who seemed unsure of where they were going. Ten minutes later, I pulled into a parking spot in front of the one story concrete and stucco structure that was still gleaming white in its newness. We hopped out of the jeep and glanced up at the sign that read *Cayman Animal Care* and nodded, liking the way it looked.

I was about to climb the short flight of steps when I caught a glimpse of something out of the corner of my eye. I stopped and turned around.

"What is it?" Josie said, following my eyes.

"Over there," I said, nodding my head in the general direction. "Somebody is watching us."

Josie stared, then frowned.

"He's got binoculars on us," she said, putting her hands on her hips.

"Yeah, so I see," I said. "That's just rude. Let's go check it out."

We both started walking across the parking lot, then the man holding the binoculars lowered them and tossed them aside. He started the car and did a quick U-turn. Soon, the car disappeared from sight.

"Weird," Josie said, glancing over at me.

"That's the word for it," I said, my neurons firing with no particular destination in mind. I shook my head to clear it. "Why would anybody be following us?"

"I have no idea," I said, heading back toward the steps, deep in thought. "Maybe he wasn't watching us."

"You think somebody might be keeping a close eye on Teresa?" Josie said.

"I guess it's possible," I said, shrugging. "But why would anybody do that? She runs an animal shelter."

"Maybe an unhappy customer?" Josie said.

"Like what? A disgruntled chicken owner?" I said, laughing.

Josie glanced back at the spot where the car had been parked. "Disgruntled. Good word." She continued to stare off into the distance deep in thought.

"What's the matter?" I said.

"I'm just wondering if gruntled is a word."

"I guess it must be, right?" I said, shrugging. "You really couldn't be disgruntled unless it was also possible to be gruntled."

"What does it mean?"

"The opposite of *dis*gruntled, I imagine."

"Thanks for clearing that up," she said, reaching for the front door. "Allow me to get the door for you. I'll be most *gruntled* to do that."

We stepped inside and glanced around the spacious registration area that was similar to the one at the Doggy Inn back home. The walls were bright white and adorned with several framed photos of animals and people enjoying their company. We heard noises coming from the back of the building, and we made our way down a hallway. We found Teresa chatting with a couple of workers who were putting the finishing touches on the section of the shelter devoted to cats. I knew this because of the sign above the door that read *Cat Land*.

My powers of deduction are matched only by my ability to read signs.

Several spacious cages, each one outfitted with a litter box and a scratching post, stretched out along one wall. There was also a common area for the cats that was basically a huge cage that contained multiple levels of resting places that would comfortably house dozens of felines.

"Hey, I didn't hear you come in," Teresa said, turning toward us. "Frank, why don't you and Wally head outside and check on the bird sanctuary? I'm expecting a couple of peacocks to be delivered soon."

"You got it," the man called Frank said. He nodded at his co-worker, and they disappeared through a door.

"Peacocks?" Josie said, raising an eyebrow at me. "Toto, I have a feeling we're not in Kansas anymore."

I laughed.

"Somebody found them on the side of the road the other night," Teresa said. "They're supposed to be pretty tame, but apparently they had a heck of a time catching them. The owner was probably someone who thought it would be a great idea to have pet peacocks, but then didn't have a clue how to take care of them."

"Or the birds lost their cool factor, and they lost interest," Josie said, shaking her head. "People do some of the strangest things when it comes to animals."

"Speaking of people doing strange things," I said. "Somebody was watching us through a pair of binoculars when we got here."

Teresa flinched then glanced back and forth at us.

"Did you get a good look at him?"

"How did you know it was a he?" I said, frowning.

"Let's call it a lucky guess," Teresa said, shaking her head. "What kind of car was it?"

"It was an old Mercedes," I said.

"A silver one?" Teresa said.

"Yeah. You know who it was, huh?" Josie said.

"My ex-husband," she said, glancing down at the floor. "He showed up a few weeks ago."

"He's been away?" I said.

"Nothing gets past you," Josie said, snorting.

"Shut it."

"Yes, he's been gone for over a year. Supposedly working on some big real estate deal in the Bahamas."

"He works in real estate?" I said.

"Man, you're on fire today," Josie said, chuckling.

"I said, shut it."

"Gavin likes to think so," Teresa said, heading for a door that had a sign on it that read *Dog World*. "He's always working on some deal he thinks is going to make him rich and famous."

"Why is he keeping an eye on you?" Josie said. "You said you've been divorced for years."

"We have," Teresa said, stepping inside the section of the shelter designated for dogs. "And he's always kept his distance. He's never even been interested in seeing his daughters."

"I'm so sorry," I said. "Your girls must be devastated by that."

"They were at one point," she said, frowning. "And we've had many tearful nights. But now, they seem to have accepted it. Or at least resigned themselves to it." She exhaled loudly and sat down on a large box. "I do my best not to trash him in front of the girls, but sometimes it's hard. How do you explain to two young girls that their father is a self-centered loser who is only concerned about himself?"

Josie and I let her question pass without comment. Teresa stood and began giving us the tour of the dog area. It was spacious, and I was impressed with how it had turned out. She then led us outside where a fenced paddock, about an acre in size, sat directly behind the shelter.

"For horses, donkeys, whatever," she said, shrugging. "And maybe the occasional pig. I'm still not sure how many large animal strays we'll get, but the girls have horses, and we couldn't leave them behind."

"It looks great," Josie said. "And you've got the contract done with Dr. Seltzer?"

"Yes, we got it done over the phone and on Skype. And she seems wonderful," Teresa said. "Where on earth did you find her?"

"I went to vet school with her. She was working in Florida, but I'd heard she wasn't very happy where she was. And as soon as I mentioned moving down here, she was all over it. You two are really going to hit it off."

"She should be here in a couple of days," Teresa said. "I can't wait to meet her." She led us to an area next to the paddock that had a massive netting over it that reminded me of a batting cage. "And this is the bird and reptile sanctuary. In my old place, people were always bringing wounded birds to me, and I felt bad that I didn't have a way to take care of them. But this should do the trick."

"It's really nice," I said, taking the space in. "You've done great work, Teresa. What do you need from us?"

"Not much, really, Suzy," she said. "You've both done so much already. But you'll be here for the grand opening, right?"

"Of course," Josie said, nodding. "We wouldn't miss it."

"Especially since it's a catered event," I said, glancing at Josie.

"Funny."

"Can I ask you why your ex-husband is keeping such a close eye on you all of a sudden?" I said.

"I think it has something to do with the fact that he showed up at your new restaurant a couple of nights ago looking for me."

"Okay," I said, frowning. I had no idea where the conversation was going. The restaurant wasn't even open for business yet.

"He came in right after the work crew went home, and Rocco and I were sitting at the bar getting...a little friendly. If you know what I mean."

"Got it," I said. "And your ex didn't like the fact that you were with another man?"

"No, not at all," Teresa said. "He flipped out, started screaming in my face, then grabbed Rocco by the arm."

"Uh-oh," Josie said.

"That was a big mistake," I said, shaking my head at Rocco's probable reaction.

"Rocco really didn't hurt him, although I didn't know an arm could bend that far without breaking," she said, grimacing at the memory. "But more than anything, Rocco *embarrassed* him. And Gavin's ego simply couldn't handle it. He left, but he made it clear that he'd be keeping a close eye on me. I've seen him lurking around a couple of times since then, but I didn't know he was hanging around the shelter."

"Would you like us to have a chat with the police?" I said. "My mother is pretty tight with them."

"No, I'd rather not at the moment," she said. "I'm sure he was just blowing off steam. Gavin's pretty harmless."

"How can you be so sure of that?" Josie said.

"Because he's always been all talk and no action," Teresa said. "And Rocco definitely made quite an impression on him."

"Yeah, Rocco's very good at that," Josie said. "But don't be shy about asking for help if you need it."

"I won't," she said, brushing her hair back and looking around. "I can't believe we're ready to open."

"The place looks amazing," I said, unable to shake the idea of Teresa being stalked by her ex-husband. "Why is he back on Grand Cayman?"

"I have no idea," she said, shrugging. "But I'm sure he's working on some deal that's *destined to bring him fame and fortune.*"

Then she laughed, but I couldn't help but notice the hint of despair that was mixed in.

"We need to get going, Teresa," I said. "We're supposed to meet my mom at the vet's office."

"Thanks for stopping by," she said. "And please thank her again for me. You guys and your mother went way overboard on the girls' presents."

"Hey, we were delighted to do it," I said. "I'm glad they enjoyed them."

"It was way too much," she said, smiling. "But thank you. By the way, was Santa good to you?"

I glanced at Josie and shook my head.

"I knew there was something we forgot to do."

Chapter 7

Dr. Yuri Wallace was a tall, jovial gentleman with a Colonel Sanders beard and a piercing look that drew you in and made you pay attention. We found him in one of the exam rooms at his clinic chatting and laughing with my mother. The King Charles Spaniel was resting comfortably on a padded exam table, and he stood and wagged his tail when we entered the room. We both said our hellos to the dog then shook hands with the elderly vet I placed anywhere between sixty and eighty. Josie and I gave my mother a hug, then sat down and looked around the room. Photos of Dr. Wallace with a wide variety of people and their pets adorned the walls, and it appeared that the smile he was giving us might be permanent.

"It's so nice to meet you," he said, glancing back and forth at us. "And I'm so sorry I couldn't make it to the barbecue yesterday. I had an emergency surgery on a Dachshund who thought it would be a good idea to pick a fight with a Blue Iguana."

I remembered reading about the native lizard that had almost become extinct but had recently been making a comeback due to the work of some organizations dedicated to saving the species.

"Gotta love the Dachshunds. Those little guys can be fearless," Josie said, shaking her head. "How big was the lizard?"

"Almost four feet," Dr. Wallace said. "Usually, the lizards will do everything they can to avoid trouble, but the dog got him cornered."

"And?" Josie said.

"And the dog almost got his face bit off," he said, shrugging. "But the Dachshund got a few good licks of his own in."

"Are they okay?" Josie said.

"I'm happy to report that both the dog and lizard are resting comfortably," he said with a booming laugh. "But in separate cages. You must be Josie Court."

"I am," she said, bowing slightly.

"I've been doing some research on you," he said, studying her closely.

"Why would you do that?" Josie said, raising an eyebrow at him

"As soon as I heard that you and Suzy, it is Suzy, right?" he said, smiling at me.

"It is," I said, returning his contagious smile.

"Your mother has told me so much about you."

"I wouldn't put too much stock in what she says, Doc. She's a drinker."

"Funny, darling."

Our banter got another burst of laughter out of him.

"As I was saying, as soon as I heard the two of you were building a new shelter, a magnificent gesture on your part, I decided to take a look into your background. It isn't often a new vet shows up, and I'm always on the lookout for talented people to help me out when I get overloaded."

"How sweet," Josie gushed.

"There's really nothing sweet about it," he said, shrugging. "You graduated top of your class, I can't even count the number of awards you've won, and you could have gone anywhere, but you decided to open your practice as part of…what do you call it, a dog hotel?"

"Doggy Inn," Josie said.

"And now you're opening an animal shelter here on Grand Cayman," he said, beaming at both of us. "You're obviously not doing that for the money. I'm impressed by that. With both of you."

Josie and I blushed. If this guy acted this way with people, I could only imagine how good he was with animals. Then he focused on the King Charles that continued to sit quietly on the table and stare up at us with those big brown eyes.

"Now, about this little guy," he said. "I think your initial observations were correct. He appears to be mildly concussed, but the good news is that I don't think his retina is detached. And his left pupil appears to be returning to normal." He rubbed the dog's head then looked at Josie. "Why did you feel the need to bring him to me?"

"I don't do much work with eyes," Josie said, suddenly uncomfortable. "And I certainly don't do eye surgery, so I thought an ophthalmologist should take a look at him. Just in case."

"I'm picking up on something," he said softly. "Why on earth would a woman with your talents avoid doing work on eyes? There's a bit more training required, but nothing that would tax your abilities."

"I just choose not to work on them," she said, tight-lipped.

"Hmmm," Dr. Wallace said.

"What's your point, Doc?" Josie said with an edge to her voice.

"I'm just wondering what happened," he said softly.

"Nothing happened," Josie snapped.

My mother and I flinched, glanced at Josie, then we locked eyes with each other and shrugged.

"I'm sorry to upset you," Dr. Wallace said, stroking the dog's fur. "You know, I remember one time when I was in school way back when. I was assisting with a spaying, and I made a mistake that almost killed the dog. It took me a long time before I was able to trust myself to do that procedure."

"Who have you been talking to, Dr. Wallace?" Josie said, glaring at him.

"I must admit that I'm very good friends with one of your former professors. Actually, I believe he's now a Dean."

"Jim Gallagher," Josie said, giving him a blank stare. "I haven't talked to him in a while. How's Jim doing?"

"He's good."

"And when you were checking up on me, he just happened to mention a little problem I had during my internship?"

"We all make mistakes, Josie," he said softly.

"I blinded that dog in one eye," Josie said, tearing up.

"You were trying to save his eyesight," he said, placing a hand on her shoulder.

"Well, I only got it half right, didn't I?"

"Jim said that you did a great job saving the other eye."

Josie shrugged and stared down at the floor.

"Treating severe glaucoma in older dogs has a low probability of success. You know that. And you should feel proud of the fact that you were able to preserve eyesight in one eye. Managing to save it in both eyes, according to Jim, would have been a miracle."

"Well, it's a little hard to save a dog's eyesight when the person responsible for saving it manages to snip the optic nerve in half," Josie said, unable to look up.

I noticed several tears beginning to drop on the linoleum floor. I started to move toward Josie to console her, but my mother stopped me with a shake of her head.

"You know, I could use a little help around the place from time to time," Dr. Wallace said. "If you're interested."

"You mean I can come in and assist you with some eye surgeries and get my confidence back?" Josie said, wiping her eyes with the back of her sleeve.

"Perhaps," he said, beaming at her.

"I'll think about it," Josie said, exhaling loudly. "Are we done here?"

"Yes, I believe we are," Dr. Wallace said. "Just keep him away from your other dogs for a few days and let him get his rest. In a couple of days, his pupil should return to normal. But if it doesn't, bring him back in and we'll take another look."

Josie nodded, gently lifted the spaniel off the table and headed for the door.

"It was nice meeting you," she managed to mumble on her way out.

"Thanks, Yuri," my mother said, placing a hand on his arm. "We'll keep a close watch on the little guy. Did her professor have anything else to say?"

"Other than saying she was the best he'd ever seen, not that much," he said, then laughed. "We spent most of the time complaining about our golf games."

My mother gave him a hug and peck on the cheek and headed for the exit. I said my goodbyes and followed her outside. Josie was sitting in the passenger seat of the jeep and nestling the King Charles in her arms.

"Not a word about it, right?" my mother said as we approached our cars parked next to each other.

"No. She'll talk about it if and when she's ready," I said, giving her a quick hug.

"That's my girl," she said, opening her car door. "Oh, I almost forgot to ask. How does the shelter look?"

"Amazing," I said, then decided to let her in on what was happening with Teresa. "But it appears that Teresa's ex-husband might be stalking her."

"Really? That's disgusting. Does Rocco know that?"

"Oh, yeah."

"Then Teresa has nothing to worry about," she said, giving me a smile as she climbed into the driver seat. "I'll see you later this afternoon. Just drop the dog off on your way back from the restaurant. And by the way, if we don't open presents soon, I'm going to start taking it very personally."

"And nobody wants that, right?" I said.

"No, darling, you most certainly do not."

Chapter 8

Josie kept to herself the entire time as we headed to the restaurant, and she stared out the window and stroked the King Charles' head, silently processing the bad memory that had resurfaced. But it became clear, despite whatever place she'd gone inside her head, she hadn't lost her touch, and by the time the short drive was over, the dog was sprawled across her lap as if in a trance.

I found her lack of banter disconcerting, almost unrecognizable, but said nothing.

I parked right in front of the freshly painted restaurant and hopped out of the jeep. I glanced up at the sign above the door and smiled at the gold *C's* written in cursive script against a dark green background. The sign looked great set against the white exterior that was trimmed with the same green that was on the sign.

"Two new signs for two new businesses in the same day," I said, glancing at her. "That's a first, huh?"

Josie nodded but said nothing. She adjusted the dog in her arms. The King Charles was alert and taking in his surroundings.

"I can't wait to check out the final menu," I said, rubbing the dog's head. "Chef Claire said she has a couple of surprises on it just for us."

Again, I got a silent nod out of her.

"I wonder if she'll make us lunch. Are you hungry?"

Josie shook her head.

Stunned by what could have been a first, I was torn between slapping her cheek to snap her out of whatever funk she'd slipped into or calling the Guinness Book of World Records.

"You're not hungry?"

She shook her head again and sighed loudly.

"That's probably a good thing. It couldn't hurt you to miss a meal or two."

She flinched, but recovered and focused on the dog.

"Okay, so you're going to play it that way, huh?" I said. "Then I'm just going to stand here and ask you a bunch of questions."

She glared at me.

"Are you sick?"

No reaction.

"Headache? Allergies? Constipated?" I said, raising an eyebrow. "Or maybe the opposite? You got tummy problems? Did something you ate last night disagree with you? Like maybe that half-gallon of ice cream."

"It wasn't a half-gallon," she whispered through clenched teeth.

"What?"

More silence.

"Homesick?"

Nothing.

"Are you bored?"

This time, I got a slow head shake out of her. Her eyes were narrowed, and I knew she was on a low boil and about to pop.

"Yearning for male companionship?" I said, grinning.

"You really are incredibly annoying."

"What?"

"You heard me."

"There's my girl," I said, offering my shoulder to her. "Go ahead. It'll make you feel better. Ow!" I rubbed my shoulder and glared at her. "I was joking."

"You're right," she deadpanned. "I do feel better."

"So, I take it you're done feeling sorry for yourself?"

"Yeah, I'm done," she said, nodding. "Sorry about that. That blast from the past just caught me by surprise."

"I know it did," I said, rubbing the dog's head. "Look at him. Those eyes just kill me."

"Yeah, he's gorgeous. And such a little lovebug."

"You were lying about not being hungry, right?"

"I could eat."

"Then let's go see what we can scrounge up in the kitchen," I said, heading up the small set of steps.

"Suzy?"

"Yeah?" I said, glancing over my shoulder.

"Thanks."

"Don't mention it," I said, smiling at her. "If I wasn't around to kick your butt every once in a while, you'd be impossible to live with."

"And for the record, it wasn't a half-gallon."

"Of course, it wasn't," I deadpanned, heading for the door. "They're on the metric system down here."

I held the door open for her, laughing the entire time, and she glared at me as she walked into the restaurant. All the windows were open in what I assumed was an attempt to remove the smell of fresh paint, and a cool breeze flowed through the dining room that dominated the space. Chef Claire and Rocco were behind the bar taking inventory, and they both looked up when they saw us.

"The place looks great," I said, looking around the dining room, now painted a light peach color. "What capacity did we end up with?"

"Sixty in the dining room," Chef Claire said. "And eight more people can eat at the bar."

"Big cnough," I said, nodding. I gave Rocco a hug and glanced around at the bar. "It looks fantastic. You been brushing up on how to make a Mudslide?"

"I can make them in my sleep," he said, laughing. "You guys want one?"

"No, thanks," I said. "I'm driving, and we need to get home and open presents or my mom is going to kill us. You ready to go, Chef Claire?"

"Yeah, I think we're done here," she said. "But hang on a sec. I want you to meet Chef Finn." She headed toward the kitchen and poked her head through the swinging door. Moments later, a short, squatty man somewhere in his forties wearing a white uniform and chef hat entered the dining room. He seemed distracted, but managed a smile and shook hands with us as Chef Claire handled the introductions.

"It's nice to finally meet you," he said in an unmistakable Australian accent. "I'd like to stay and chat, but I've got a stack of fresh snapper and wahoo to clean and gut."

"Yuk," I said, frowning.

"That's right," Chef Finn said. "You must be the one who doesn't eat fish, right?"

"Guilty as charged," I said, shrugging.

"Well, I'm gonna change your mind about that," he said, grinning at me. "I do a smoked wahoo you'd swear comes straight from a Thanksgiving turkey."

"I'll take your word for it," I said, grimacing.

"I love fresh snapper," Josie said, softly clapping her hands. "How are you preparing it?"

"You must be the snacker," Chef Finn said, giving Josie the once-over. "We're doing it three ways."

Josie thought for a moment.

"Well, you must be doing a baked snapper."

"We are. Whole fish. And baked on a bed of potatoes, carrots, and onions. A touch of garlic and a rosemary-thyme-paprika rub."

"Sounds amazing," Josie said, nodding.

"It serves two," Chef Finn said.

"Don't bet on it," Chef Claire said, laughing.

"Funny," Josie said, then refocused. "Sauteed?"

"Yup. In garlic butter and lemon. Served with a side of saffron rice with sultanas and a chilled cucumber and onion salad. Chef Claire and I put a lot of thought into that one."

"Simple but elegant," Chef Claire said, beaming at her colleague.

"Perfect," Josie said. "Let's see…one more. Dare I hope to dream that it might be deep-fried?"

"You're good," he said, laughing. "Caribbean-style fish and chips. We're offering it on the main menu, but we expect to move a ton of it on the takeout side of the house. What do you think?"

"I think I love you," Josie said, apparently fully recovered from her earlier bout of depression.

Chef Finn playfully waved her away then said his goodbyes and headed back into the kitchen. Chef Claire and Josie, carrying the King Charles, headed outside. I remained behind to talk with Rocco.

"What's up?" he said, sitting down on one of the barstools.

"Teresa's ex-husband was sitting outside the shelter earlier. He had binoculars on Josie and me when we got there."

"Did he say anything?" Rocco said, his eyes narrowing.

"No, we headed his way, but he drove off before we could get close."

"I guess the guy doesn't know the meaning of get lost," he said, cracking his knuckles.

I assumed it was a holdover from his previous line of work. If it was, it was a good choice. It certainly got my attention.

"What are you going to do?" I said.

"It looks like I'm going to have to make my point a bit more forcefully," he said as casually as he might sound ordering a sandwich.

"Do you think he's dangerous?" I said, studying him closely.

"Only to himself," he said, standing up. "Don't worry about him, Suzy. I'll handle this."

"You're not going to hurt him are you?"

"That's completely up to him."

"Please don't do anything crazy, Rocco," I said.

"You mean, like kill him?" he said, grinning at me.

"Actually, I was thinking more along the lines of a punch in the nose, but, yeah, let's go with the killing thing."

Rocco laughed.

"Seriously, Rocco. You don't want any issues with the cops down here. I know your prior record is ancient history, but it could come back to haunt you in a hurry if you assault one of the locals. Please be careful."

"The guy's a total loser, Suzy," Rocco said. "He's completely ignored those two beautiful girls for years. And now he's stalking Teresa."

"Yes, I know he is," I said. "But let's see if we can just strongly *suggest* he takes a hike, okay?"

"I'll do my best," he said. "But like I said, that's going to be his call."

"Okay, point taken," I said, getting to my feet. "You and Teresa seem really happy."

"We're unbelievably happy. In fact, I need to talk with you guys about me staying down here year-round."

"Really?" I said, surprised.

"You'll need someone to manage this place when you guys aren't around, right?"

"We will," I said, nodding. "But we'd sure miss you if you weren't in Clay Bay."

"Not as much as I'd miss her and the kids," he said softly.

"Yeah, I get that," I said, nodding. "You're a lucky man, Rocco."

"Luck has nothing to do with it. Actually, I'm blessed."

"Blessed are the meek?" I said, grinning.

"First time I've ever been called that," he said, laughing. "And I sure don't want to inherit the earth."

"Just your own little slice of heaven, right?"

"Exactly."

"And now that you found it, you'll do everything necessary to preserve and protect it."

"Nothing gets past you."

Chapter 9

Surrounded by seven dogs, we finally got around to opening presents after dinner. Fortunately, our mutual pledge not to go overboard on gifts to each other held, but we all failed miserably when it came to the dogs. I won't bother to list the multitude and wide variety of presents our dogs received. Let's just say that Santa was very good to all of them and leave it at that. We were even able to redirect a few gifts to the King Charles so he wouldn't feel left out. He spent the entire time on my mother's lap holding one of the toys he'd gotten in his mouth. His eye had continued to improve, and we were happy to see that his balance seemed better and he was no longer bumping into every object he crossed paths with. But he did manage to get one of my mother's oven mitts stuck on his head. We're still not sure how he managed to pull that one off.

"What are we going to do about this guy?" my mother said, stroking the King Charles' head.

"I called the hospital this afternoon and got the address the woman gave them before she was discharged," I said as I watched Chloe and Captain try to decide which of the two identical toys each one wanted.

"Is it a local address?" Josie said, laughing as Chloe tugged on one of Captain's ears until he dropped the toy he was playing keep away with.

"Yeah. It's somewhere off South Sound Road," I said, shaking my head at my Aussie as she terrorized Captain, who was over twice her size. "Geez, Chloe, take it easy. You're lucky he's easygoing. I thought I'd swing by the address in the morning and check it out."

"Don't forget to ask about the dog's name," Josie said. "Pretty soon the little guy is going to start thinking his name is *Who's a good boy*."

"Will do," I said, nodding. "You want to come along?"

"No, I thought I'd do a few projects around the house in the morning. Then I'm going to hang out by the pool and try to catch up on some email. I'm way behind."

"I'd go, but I need to be at the restaurant all day," Chef Claire said. "Opening night."

"What time should we be there?" my mother said.

"Seven would be good," Chef Claire said. "We'll have your table ready to go."

"Who's going to be at dinner with us?" I said to my mother.

"Let's see," she said, gently stroking the King Charles' head. "The three of us, of course. And Gerald will be there with his new girlfriend."

"What does she do?" Josie said.

"According to Gerald, not as much as he would like," my mother said, giving us a coy smile.

"Poor Gerald," I said, shaking my head.

"But I think she's in finance. Maybe a banker."

"Now there's a shock," I said, shaking my head. "Every other person I meet down here seems to work in finance."

"Well, darling, one has to go where the money is," my mother deadpanned. "Get it?"

"Yeah, got it, Mom."

"And Dr. Couch will be there. You remember him from the barbecue. And he's bringing one of his business associates. Who am I forgetting?" She thought for a moment. "Oh, of course, Teresa. She got a sitter for the girls. And since Rocco will be working, we couldn't let her eat dinner by herself."

"You decided what you're going to have yet?" Chef Claire said to Josie.

"I'm still going back and forth," she said. "But it will definitely be something from the snapper family."

"I'm going with a steak," I said.

"Philistine," my mother said.

"Thanks, Mom," I said, making a face at her. "Oh, I almost forgot to tell you. Rocco told me that he's thinking about moving here on a year-round basis."

"Wow," Josie said. "That was fast."

"He's been dropping some hints for a while," Chef Claire said. "I don't have any problem with it. We're going to need a manager for the restaurant. Finn is great, but he hates dealing with anything outside of the kitchen."

"And Rocco brings his considerable bartending skills with him," Josie said, then grinned. "Not to mention crowd control."

"Who have we got at home that could handle being bar manager at C's?" I said.

"At the moment," Chef Claire said. "I don't think we have anybody."

"We've got lots of time," Josie said. "We'll figure it out. We always do."

"To us," my mother said, raising her champagne flute in a toast.

We clinked glasses, wished each other Merry Christmas again, then cleaned up the mess we'd made opening presents. The three of us walked down the beach toward the house lugging our individual Christmas bounty with the dogs leading the way. We put everything away then sat around the pool doing our best to stay dry as the dogs climbed in and out of the pool. They took great pains to shake as close to us as possible, then we gave up all hope of remaining dry, changed into our swimsuits, and joined them for a late-night swim.

As days went, this one was pretty much off the charts. Apart from learning that Teresa's ex-husband was back in the picture and might try to make life difficult for her, everything was going to plan and was right on schedule. And if I was able to track down the owner of the King Charles, tomorrow had the potential to be even better.

But a thought continued to nag at me as I did my best to swim a lap with four hovering dogs who were either trying to help me make it across the pool or drown me in the deep end.

Owen.

Who the heck is Owen?

Chapter 10

I ate breakfast with Chef Claire that, due to the crunch of the Granola she'd made, turned into a noisy affair that had the dogs on point and was probably loud enough to wake Josie from a sound sleep. The slices of fresh mango were quieter but just as delicious, and I pushed my plate away, full and ready to give my full attention to a second cup of coffee I'd poured into a traveler mug.

"It's so easy to eat healthy down here," I said, taking a careful sip.

"Concur," Chef Claire said, slurping down a slice of mango. "Unless you're counting the bite-sized."

"I count most of them. And they're so small," I said, laughing. "This mango is fantastic."

"We should plant some fruit trees in the yard."

"That's a great idea," I said, sliding off my stool and grabbing my car keys. "I'll see you tonight. I'd wish you good luck with the opening, but you're not going to need it. It's gonna be great."

"Thanks. Be safe out there today," she said, raising an eyebrow.

"Safe? Why wouldn't I be safe?"

"Because you're about to start snooping," she said. "And we all know how that usually goes."

"O ye of little faith," I said, gently punching her on the arm and heading for the garage.

I drove down the driveway, made my way south on Seven Mile Road and wound my way onto South Sound Road. I slowed as I kept an eye out for the side street I was looking for. Then I made a left and soon found myself in front of a traditional Cayman house made of wood and painted pink and green. It was highlighted by a massive porch that stretched the width of the structure. I hopped out of the jeep and made my way through the landscaped path that led to a set of steps. A small sign reading *Sylvia's Guesthouse* was attached to the railing.

I knocked and waited.

A large woman with gray hair tied back in a bun opened the door and smiled at me.

"Good morning," she said. "How can I help you?"

"Hi, are you Sylvia?"

"I am," she said, patiently waiting for me to continue.

"My name is Suzy Chandler. And I'm looking for someone."

"Okay," she said, shrugging. "Who are you looking for?"

"Well, you see, that's the hard part. I don't know her name."

"That might make it a bit more difficult to find her," she said, chuckling.

"Yeah, it's kind of a strange situation," I said.

I spent a few minutes explaining the water rescue on Christmas morning and how the hospital had given me her address. She listened carefully, occasionally nodding as I continued.

"Isn't it a bit strange that the hospital had my address, but didn't get her name?"

"I was thinking the same thing," I said, nodding. "But she was basically unconscious when she was admitted, and before they were willing to discharge her, she had to prove she was able to answer some basic questions. You know name and address. How old are you? Stuff like that. And the only name the nurses could remember her giving was Bobbie. No last name. And one of the nurses said she might have been lying about her name."

"That's odd," Sylvia said. "What does she look like?"

"Attractive, average height, long light brown hair turning blonde from the sun, somewhere in her thirties."

"Yes, I think I know who you're talking about. But she told me her name was Vera. No last name," she said, stepping out onto the porch and closing the door behind her. She gestured at two chairs sitting nearby. "Let's enjoy this beautiful morning before it gets too hot, shall we?"

"What was she like?" I said, sitting down in a chair next to her.

"She was a pleasant young woman. Very respectful and quiet as a mouse. For someone in my business, the perfect house guest. But she seemed…troubled."

"How so?" I said as my Snoopmeter turned itself on.

"It was like she was always on guard. You know, on the lookout for somebody who might be watching her."

"Afraid?"

"No, I wouldn't say afraid," she said, frowning. "It was more like cautious. Almost like she was a spy or something. But I'm sure that's just me reading too much into it. I watch way too many spy movies."

"Sure, sure," I said, nodding. "I'm the same way with cop shows. How long was she here?"

"She stayed for about a week," Sylvia said. "Then one morning she paid her bill in cash and left."

"When did she leave?"

"It was two days before Christmas. I remember because I always make a big Christmas dinner for all my guests, and I asked her if she'd be coming. Can I ask why you're looking for her?"

"I have her dog," I said, shrugging. "And I'd like to give him back to her."

"You have Earl?"

"That's his name? Earl?"

"Yes, she told me the name was a playful reference to the King Charles. You know, Earl, as in the royal title."

"Cool name," I said. "Now we know what to call him. Thanks. That helps."

She noticed the deep frown on my face.

"What's wrong?"

"When she was discharged from the hospital she didn't try to find the dog," I said, shaking my head. "She wouldn't have known who to talk to, but she could have asked all the people who live near the beach where she was rescued. There aren't that many of us."

"You live on Seven Mile Beach?"

"Yes," I said.

"Nice," she said, staring off into the distance with a smile on her face. "I used to be a housekeeper over there. But only until I'd saved enough money to open this place." Then she stared at me, confused. "Are you sure you're okay?"

"The fact that she didn't try to find Earl is really bothering me," I said.

"Well, she adored that dog and never went anywhere without him. And she did say she was planning to go somewhere far away. Now, I'm worried that something bad might have happened to her."

"But you don't know of anyone who might have been looking for her?"

"No," Sylvia said. "Apart from a few conversations she had with some of the other guests over dinner, I never saw her talk to anyone. Except for Earl. She chatted with him all the time."

"He's a cute dog," I said.

"And he was also rescued by your dog?"

"He was. Actually, Captain belongs to my best friend," I said. "But on most days, I think we pretty much belong to them."

"He sounds like a very special animal."

"He is," I said, nodding. "Did she ever mention anyone by the name of Owen?"

"No," she said, shaking her head. "That doesn't ring a bell at all. Would you like something to drink?"

"No, thank you," I said, getting up. "I need to run. But thanks so much for your help."

"You're very welcome," she said, also standing and extending her hand. "It was nice meeting you. Good luck. And I hope she's okay. But if you don't find her and need a place for the dog, just let me know. I'd be delighted to look after him."

"I'll keep that in mind," I said, shaking her hand.

Over my mother's dead body, I thought, hiding a smile.

I made my way down the path and hopped into the jeep and headed for home.

Now that it had been confirmed that the mysterious Vera-Bobbie was officially a dog lover, my neurons started churning. I had to agree with Sylvia's concern that something bad might have happened to the woman. But I was at a complete loss about what to do next. I couldn't go to the police and file a missing person report on an unnamed woman just because she'd left her dog behind.

On the surface, there was nothing particularly special about the mysterious woman's situation. Travelers of all types and ages come and go through the islands of the Caribbean on a constant basis: Tourists and trekkers, con artists and schemers, retirees and ex-pats, and a host of other people looking to escape the brutal northern winters, or just looking to escape. Then she'd gotten into trouble on the water and had to be rescued. It happened all the time.

And she may have had a very good reason for leaving her King Charles behind. But that idea nagged and cut deep into my thoughts. Sylvia's comment about how cautious the woman was, and how it appeared she was constantly on the lookout for someone who might be watching her wouldn't go away.

Then some neurons collided and a lightbulb popped in my head.

I pulled the jeep over, made a U-turn and headed back to Sylvia's. She was surprised to see me when she opened the door.

"Did you forget something?" she said.

"I'm sorry to bother you. But you mentioned that the only conversations Vera had were with some of your other guests."

"Yes, that's right," she said, confused. "What about it?"

"Was one of the guests a man called Gavin?"

"Why, yes. As a matter of fact, it was. A good-looking man, dark hair, around forty? Rather ill-tempered?"

"I don't know," I said, shrugging. "I've never met him."

"Okay," she said, now baffled.

"Is he still staying here?"

"No, he checked out yesterday."

"Did he happen to mention where he was going?" I said.

"No, he didn't. All he said was that he had some business to attend to that would take him out of town for a while."

"Thanks, Sylvia," I said, staring off into the distance.

She must have gotten concerned because I only came back to the present when I felt her gentle hand on my arm.

"Are you okay, Suzy?"

"Sure, I'm fine. Why do you ask?"

"You just seemed to drift off for a while," she said, chuckling.

"Oh, that," I said, waving it off. "Don't worry about that. It happens all the time."

"Don't you think you're a bit young to be having a senior moment?" she said, laughing.

"Actually, I think it's more of an occupational hazard," I said, smiling at her.

"Are you a cop?"

"No, I run an inn for dogs," I said, again staring off.

"Not to sound alarming, dear, but you might want to stay out of the sun for a few days."

I grinned at her and waved goodbye then hopped back into the jeep. Teresa's ex-husband, the stalker, knew the mysterious Vera-Bobbie who had disappeared from sight. It wasn't much to go on, but it was certainly more than I'd started the day with. As

I headed for home, I mulled over my options about how to track down the driver of the silver Mercedes with an apparent fondness for binoculars and have a little chat with him under the guise of reuniting the woman with her beloved dog, Earl.

Earl.

Cool name for a cool little dog.

Chapter 11

I was halfway through my dinner, doing my best to feign interest in the conversations about asset-turnover ratio, cash reserve ratio, and capital adequacy ratio that were dominating the table. I didn't have a clue what my mother and her dinner guests were talking about, but I did manage to glean that ratios must be important when it comes to the world of high finance. Fortunately, Dr. Couch, who was an avid collector of antiques, started talking about a set of 18th century chairs he'd just bought at auction. Normally, talking about chairs is about as interesting as watching paint dry, but after my forced finance lesson, I found the conversation about the beauty and durability of Cuban mahogany a most welcome change.

I was about to take another bite of my steak when I saw a man enter the restaurant by himself and take a seat at the bar. Rocco glanced up from the conversation he was having with a couple sitting at the bar and immediately went on point. But he remained calm, walked over to the man, and placed a menu in front of him. Rocco turned around briefly to pour the man a beer, then took his order, and walked back down the bar to resume his conversation. But he kept glancing over and keeping a very close eye on the man who had his back to the dining room and was sipping his beer.

I caught Rocco's eye, and he gave me a small nod. Teresa was sitting next to me, and I nudged her and nodded in Rocco's direction. Teresa beamed at him and waved, then flinched when she saw the man sitting by himself at the bar. On cue, the man swiveled around in his seat and made eye contact with Teresa and stared hard.

"That's your ex-husband, isn't it?" I whispered.

"Yes," she said, her eyes still locked on her ex. "What on earth is he doing here?"

"Probably trying to ruin your night," I said. "So, let's not give him the satisfaction."

"What's going on?" Josie said, glancing up from her plate.

"Teresa's ex is sitting at the bar."

Josie casually glanced over in the general direction then went back to her snapper. My mother, as she always did, picked up on the atmospheric change at the table and gave me a quizzical look. I shook my head, and she let it go. But Dr. Couch sitting on the other side of Teresa leaned forward and spoke in a low voice.

"Is everything okay?"

"I think so," Teresa whispered. "My ex-husband is here."

Dr. Couch followed her eyes to the bar then frowned.

"Gavin is your ex-husband?" he said, surprised.

"Yes. You know him?" Teresa said.

"Yes, unfortunately, I do," Dr. Couch said, setting his knife and fork down. "A few years ago, he was involved in a few real estate projects I was participating in. And he's recently come back to the islands. How close are you to your ex-husband?"

"Not at all," Teresa said. "To be honest, I consider him a blight on society. Why do you ask?"

"Because I don't have anything good to say about him. If the two of you were close, I would just keep my mouth shut."

"Nothing good to say, huh?" Teresa said, sneaking a quick glance at the bar.

"Uh, no," Dr. Couch said.

"You mentioned he was involved in a couple of development deals," I said, leaning forward.

"Actually, Gavin's involvement was pretty much relegated to the sidelines. He's a bit of a..."

"Sycophantic weasel?" Teresa said.

"That works," Dr. Couch said as he picked up his knife and fork and nudged the man sitting next to him.

The man who'd been introduced as Mr. Smith and had barely spoken a word all throughout dinner paused long enough to look up and glance across the room at Teresa's ex-husband. He seemed to frown briefly when the face registered, then went back to his dinner. I assumed he was familiar with Gavin as well, and, like Dr. Couch, wasn't impressed by what he'd seen. My mother gave me another quizzical look, and I shook my head again. She frowned at me, obviously annoyed that she was missing something, but said nothing.

Then Teresa froze in her seat. I glanced at her before turning around to see her ex-husband making his way toward our table.

"Here comes the floor show," I said to Josie.

"What?" she said with a frown when I broke her mealtime focus. She glanced over her shoulder then put her utensils down and wiped her mouth. "If this guy ruins dessert, he's a dead man."

"Hello, Teresa," the man said, coming to a stop right behind my chair.

"Gavin," Teresa said in a controlled tone.

"I was wondering if I could speak with you," he said, nodding at some of the other people around the table.

"I'm right in the middle of dinner, Gavin. And we really don't have anything to talk about."

"That's where you're wrong, Teresa. We need to talk."

"No, we don't," Teresa snapped.

The rest of the table stopped what they were doing and fell silent. Some of the people at nearby tables were also paying close attention to what was playing out a few feet away.

"Uh, hi, Gavin," Gerald said, trying to sound upbeat.

"Hello, Gerald," Gavin said. "I'm sorry to interrupt your dinner, but I need a word with my ex-wife."

"Why don't you just save it for another time?" Gerald said. "This probably isn't the best place for that."

"Why don't you let me worry about that?" Gavin said, glaring at the Finance Minister. "Hello, Dr. Couch. Nice to see you again. I see you're still traveling in the right circles."

"Gavin," Dr. Couch said, nodding at the man who now had his hand on the back of my chair. "I think you should take Gerald's advice. This really isn't the time or place."

"Free advice from a doctor," Gavin said, grinning. "Now I've seen everything. Why don't you take two of these and call me in the morning?" He flashed an obscene gesture with his free hand and laughed at his own joke.

"Please take your hand off my chair," I said, glancing over my shoulder at him.

"What?" Gavin said, barely acknowledging my presence.

"Your hand. Get it off my chair," I said.

"Who is this man?" my mother said, glancing around the table.

"He's my ex-husband," Teresa said.

"Oh, the stalker," my mother said, giving him the once over before dismissing him.

"And you're obviously someone who doesn't know how to mind her own business," Gavin said, focusing on my mother. "Hey, I recognize you. You're the rich one who likes to work behind the scenes, aren't you?"

"Who I am is none of your business," my mother snapped.

"Yeah, I know who you are," Gavin said with a sneer. "Just another slimy northern carpetbagger. Ow! What the…"

He dropped to one knee and grimaced before getting back on his feet. He examined the four impressions my fork had left on his lower thigh just below where his shorts ended. I'd drawn blood, and I stared at the fork I was still holding.

"Nice shot," Josie said, glancing at the four trickles of blood that were dripping down the man's leg.

"I'm going to need a new fork," I said, glancing around for one of the servers.

It had been a backhanded jab, a reflex reaction on my part for the way he'd insulted my mother, and I sat slightly hunched over anticipating a retaliatory strike. But before Gavin could turn his anger in my direction, I heard him groan. I turned around in my chair and saw Rocco with one hand on the back of the man's shorts. The other was sunk into Gavin's neck the way an eagle might sink its talons into prey. Rocco lifted the man, wheeled around on his heels, and marched him toward the exit, using Gavin's head to open the front door. We heard the faint sounds of blows and muffled grunts followed by the sound of a car door slamming shut three times. I assumed that one or more of Gavin's body parts had prevented the door from closing the first two times.

The clamor was followed by the sound of a car engine starting then driving away. I wondered how it was possible for Gavin to be in any shape to drive, but perhaps Rocco's encouragement had been enough for the man to rise to the occasion. The restaurant patrons went back to what they were doing before the outburst, and a few minutes later I noticed that Rocco was back at work. He must have entered through the kitchen, and he seemed completely at ease chatting and laughing with the people sitting on the other side of the bar.

"Are you okay?" I said to the still rattled Teresa.

"I'll be fine," she said, exhaling loudly. "Wow, that escalated in a hurry."

"It certainly did," Dr. Couch said. Then he leaned forward to speak to me. "What did you do?"

"Stabbed him with my fork," I said, casually shrugging. "He got off easy."

"How's that?" Dr. Couch said, frowning.

"He could have been standing behind Josie," I said, laughing.

"Don't start," she said, grinning. "But I have to give you credit. Nice backhand."

"Thanks," I said. "It was a pretty easy shot."

"Ah, dang it," Dr. Couch said, staring down at his phone.

"What's the matter?" I said.

"I'm needed at the hospital," he said, getting up from his chair. "It's always something." He gave my mother a kiss on the cheek then glanced around the table. "I'm sorry to do this, but one of my patients has taken a turn for the worse. Thanks so much for dinner. It was nice seeing you all."

He waved goodbye and headed for the front door. The dinner chatter picked up where it had left off, and I got up from my chair.

"I'll be back in a minute," I said to Josie. "And don't you dare eat my dessert."

I headed for the bar and sat down at the far end. Rocco approached with a sheepish grin.

"Sorry about that," he said. "But I couldn't resist."

"Don't apologize," I said, waving it off. "You handled it perfectly. Did I hear the car door slam three times?"

"Yeah," he said, frowning. "I had a little trouble getting it closed."

"Because…?" I said, already wondering about the possibility of our getting slapped with a lawsuit on opening night.

"The first time his shoulder got in the way," Rocco said, shrugging. "The second time was his head."

"And he was still able to drive away?" I said, surprised.

"Oh, no," Rocco said, shaking his head. "I was driving the car. I didn't want to leave him out front and give our dinner guests the wrong impression. You know, a bleeding guy in the parking lot." He gave me a big grin. "No, he's in no shape to drive. I parked the car behind the restaurant. When he comes to, he'll eventually figure out a way to drive himself home."

"Did he say anything to you?" I said.

"Yeah, a few things," he said with a small shrug. "*Please. Please, no. I'm sorry.* And there were several grunts and groans tossed into the mix."

I tried not to laugh but failed miserably.

"Do you think he'll come back?"

"To the restaurant?" Rocco said. "I seriously doubt it. And if you see him hanging around anywhere near Teresa or the kids, you let me know right away. Got it?"

"Got it."

"Nice work with the fork."

"Thanks. Just a lucky shot," I said, frowning.

"What's the matter?" Rocco said, then gestured to a patron that he would be right there.

"It's just that I was hoping to have a word with the guy. I think he knows the woman Captain rescued on the beach. And we still have her dog."

"Well, whenever you're ready to have a chat with him, let me know. I want to be there with you."

"Just to encourage him to talk, right?" I said, raising an eyebrow.

"Sure," Rocco said, nodding. "I'll even help him get into his car."

Chapter 12

Things settled down soon after the encounter, and we were
able to enjoy our dessert in peace. An hour and a half later, we
were still sitting at the table in the otherwise empty restaurant.
Chef Claire and Finn joined us after the kitchen closed, and they
were drinking wine and basking in the glow of a very successful
opening night.

That is if we didn't count the guy who was probably still
bleeding all over the front seat of his car in the parking lot
behind the restaurant.

I'd changed seats and spent the last hour sitting between my
mother and the now lubricated and suddenly chatty Mr. Smith. I
learned he was originally from somewhere in Europe, actual
country of birth undisclosed, and that he was a heavy hitter when
it came to big development deals around the globe. McMansions
surrounded by golf courses and man-made lakes seemed to be a
specialty of his, and he wasn't shy about letting me know he was
on a first-name basis with several pro golfers. References to
Jack, Tiger, and Arnie – rest his soul – were liberally sprinkled
through his stories, but when I asked him what he was working
on at the moment, he fell silent and gave me a small frown.

"Not much, really," he said, eventually.

Even though I might still be a bit of a financial neophyte, I'm pretty good at recognizing a lie when I hear one. I seriously doubted a day passed when this guy spent his time doing *not much*. But if he didn't feel like sharing the specifics of his latest deal, that was fine with me. I'd heard more about eight-bedroom McMansion floor plans and the difficulties of maintaining bentgrass greens in hot climates I'd ever dreamed possible. And it was more than enough to last me a lifetime.

"Do you live here during the winter?" I said.

"I used to have a place on Seven Mile Beach, but I unloaded it a few years ago," he said, taking a gulp of wine.

"John used to own the place two doors down from me, darling."

John Smith?

I pondered the name. I'd always heard it was one of the most common names, but I was pretty sure the John Smith sitting across the table from me was the first one I'd ever actually met. The moniker was also used in the UK, in much the same way as John Doe is used in the States to describe an unknown man or as a placeholder name for an unidentified corpse. If this guy was going to the trouble of using an alias to conceal his true identity, he certainly wasn't demonstrating a lot of creativity. Unless the guy was trying to be too clever by half, I decided that John Smith probably was his actual name.

"Darling?"

"What?" I said, catching the odd look she was giving me.

"Are you still with us?" she said, laughing.

"Of course," I said, flushing red with embarrassment. "I was just trying to picture the house Mr. Smith was talking about." I turned to him. "The big white one with the gigantic pool in front?"

"That's the one," he said. "Nice house. But somebody made me an offer I couldn't refuse so…"

He gave me a smile that let me know he was sure I understood completely, and there was no need to finish the sentence for me.

"Sure, sure," I said, nodding sagely.

My mother snorted softly and laughed.

"Shut it, Mom."

Then we heard a blood-curdling scream coming from the back of the restaurant. I followed Chef Claire and Finn into the kitchen, then raced out the back door. Teresa was standing next to the silver Mercedes with the driver side door open. The overhead light inside was on, and she was staring into the car with a look of disbelief. The rest of the dinner guests had made their way outside and, as a group, we slowly made our way toward the Mercedes. I leaned forward and glanced down into the car, then grimaced and shook my head as I looked away.

"Oh, my word," my mother said, then also turned away.

Gerald approached the car, knelt down to examine the body, then stood and softly closed the door. The overhead light went dark. He removed his phone from his pocket and placed a call.

"Dead?" Josie said, not looking into the car.

"Yeah," I whispered.

"From the beating Rocco gave him?" Josie said, frowning.

"No, from the two bullets he got in the back of the head," I said, exhaling loudly.

"He got shot?" Josie said, barely managing to avoid taking a peek inside the car.

"Yeah, and given the lack of external head trauma, my guess is that the shooter used a twenty-two. Effective at close range and very quiet. Just walk up to the car, pop, pop, then walk away. Easy as falling off a log."

My mother stared at me in disbelief.

"What?" I said.

"Where on earth did that come from?"

"Hey, if you're around enough of these things, eventually you're gonna learn some stuff," I said, shrugging.

Teresa slowly trudged toward us with tears in her eyes. I gave her a long hug.

"Are you okay?" I whispered into her ear.

"I don't think so," she said, trembling. "I can't believe it. I came outside to see how he was doing and found him slumped down in his seat. Then I saw the pool of blood. So much blood."

She began shaking, and I squeezed her tight.

"Why did you feel the need to check on him?" John Smith said.

"Because he was the father of my children," Teresa snapped as she glared at him.

"Sorry," he said. "Of course. That makes perfect sense. I'm sorry."

"I know that Rocco was only trying to protect me, but I was worried he might have gone too far," Teresa said.

"I'm sure Rocco knows when to stop," I said, glancing around. "That's odd."

"What?" Josie said, following my eyes.

"Where is Rocco?"

"No, that's not possible," Teresa said, sensing where I might be headed with the conversation. She nodded at her dead ex-husband. "Rocco would never throw away what we have on that loser."

The look of hatred in her eyes was unmistakable, but no matter where my mind tried to take me, I just couldn't picture Teresa as someone capable of shooting anyone, including her stalking ex-husband. We went back inside and waited for the police and ambulance to arrive. Thankfully, Rocco was back behind the bar restocking the coolers. When we all walked back into the dining room, he paused to look up and chuckle.

"There you are," he said. "I was wondering where the heck you guys went."

Teresa approached him and gave him a long hug. She whispered in his ear, and he flinched, took a step back, and stared at her. If he was faking his surprise at hearing the news about the dead guy in the Mercedes, he was doing a great job.

"That's a relief," Josie said, studying Rocco's expression.

"No kidding," I said, nodding. "He didn't kill him."

"Think the cops will believe it?" she said, glancing at me.

"Now that's a very good question."

"Thanks. So, now we wait, right?" Josie said, shaking her head. "Again."

"Yeah, time to spend a couple of hours with a new batch of cops," I said, sitting down on one of the barstools and reaching for a couple of glasses and a half-full bottle of wine. "Are you ready to do this?"

"Sure, I've got nothing to worry about," she said. "You're the one who stabbed him with a fork."

Chapter 13

The initial investigation into the shooting was led by Detective Renfro, someone we'd gotten to know during our last visit to Grand Cayman when one of my mother's dinner guests had gotten stabbed in the chest with a metal skewer more commonly used for shish kebabs. The detective was a thorough and professional cop and had impressed us with his pleasant personality. He'd also been smitten with Chef Claire as soon as he met her and had asked her out to dinner. Chef Claire had willingly agreed, but he'd permanently ruined his chances with her when he began talking about marriage and the prospect of their having half a dozen kids before they'd gotten through the salad course. As such, their dating history, while memorable, was brief.

But he didn't seem to have taken her rejection too personally, and he was interviewing her and Chef Finn with a smile on his face as he jotted down their responses. When he finished with them, he headed for Josie and me still sitting at the end of the bar closest to the door.

"It's nice to see you, Detective Renfro," I said, extending my hand.

"Hello, Suzy. Josie," he said, nodding at both of us. "Here we go again, huh?"

"Yeah, here we go again," I said, shrugging.

He pulled up a chair and sat down between us. He flipped his notepad to a fresh page, checked his watch, and got started.

"Where were you when you heard the scream?"

I pointed into the dining room.

"I was sitting at that table having dessert."

"Were you also sitting at the table, Josie?"

"I was."

"And what were you doing at the time?"

"Is that a trick question, Detective?" Josie said.

"What?"

"I was eating dessert. What else would I be doing?" she said, flashing him a coy smile.

"I have no idea," he said, shaking his head. "That's why I asked the question." He scribbled in his notebook. "Okay, let's move on. Who was the first person to find the body?"

"Teresa," I said. "By the time we all got outside, she was already standing next to the car."

"I see. And what was she doing at the time?"

"Grieving, primarily," I said with a shrug.

"Did you see her try to move the body?"

"No."

"Touch it in any way?"

"No."

"I see. Did you hear any gunshots?"

"No," I said, shaking my head. "But I imagine that was because the shooter used a low caliber. Probably a twenty-two."

"Interesting. Why do you say that?"

"Because nobody heard a gunshot," I said.

"Hard to argue with your logic," Josie deadpanned.

"Unassailable, right?" I said, grinning at her.

"Are you two enjoying yourself?" Detective Renfro said, glancing back and forth at us.

"Yeah, as far as cop interviews go, this one's not bad," Josie said, nodding.

"Yeah, I'm good with it, too. Please, continue, Detective."

He took a deep breath and fiddled with his pen as he composed himself.

"Did you see what happened earlier when the man named Rocco had the confrontation with the victim?"

"Yes, we were both right in the middle of it," I said. "He came over to our table, got offensive with several of our guests, then Rocco *escorted* him outside."

"I heard he used the victim's head to open the door," Detective Renfro said, his pen at the ready.

"Yes, I think he may have bumped his head on the way out," I said. "But by that time, I really wasn't paying close attention."

"Why not?" he said, staring at me.

"Because she was looking for a place to hide the weapon," Josie said, laughing.

"Shut it."

"Weapon? What weapon are you talking about?" Detective Renfro said, inching forward in his seat.

"It was a fork," I said, glaring at Josie. "And I wasn't trying to hide it. I was looking for a clean one."

"A fork?" he said, listening carefully.

"Yes, he was standing behind my chair totally invading my personal space, and then he insulted my mother. I had a reflex response and backhanded my fork into his thigh."

"That explains the wound on his leg," Detective Renfro said, scribbling a note. "One of my colleagues initially thought that the actual cause of death might have been from being bitten twice by a poisonous snake."

"Instead of the two bullet holes in the back of his head?" I said, frowning.

"What can I say?" Detective Renfro said, shrugging. "He's new."

"Sure, sure."

"What can you tell me about the victim's relationship with his ex-wife?"

"Not a lot," Josie said. "But it was pretty clear that he'd been stalking her the past several days."

"Did the ex-wife tell you this?" he said, scribbling away.

"Yes," I said. "But we witnessed it ourselves. Yesterday. And, of course, tonight here at the restaurant."

"And I assume that Rocco was also aware of the man's stalking?"

"I'm sure he was," I said, nodding. "But he'll be able to better answer that question for himself."

"Yes, I'm sure he will," he said, sliding his pen back into his pocket and closing his notepad.

"Is that all?" Josie said.

"For now, yes."

"So, we can go home?" I said, getting off the stool to stretch.

"I don't see why not," he said.

"How long is the place going to remain a crime scene?" I said.

"Is that a problem?"

"Well, kinda," I said, frowning at him. "We're trying to run a restaurant here."

"You should be okay," he said, getting to his feet. "If it's still a crime scene tomorrow, we'll do our best to confine it to the area behind the restaurant. Thanks for your time, ladies. Despite the circumstances, it was a pleasure seeing you again."

"You too, Detective," I said. "By the way, how is your search for a wife going?"

"Very well," he said, smiling. "I'm getting quite serious with a lovely woman from Little Cayman. She has fourteen brothers and sisters, and twins run in the family. I'm very optimistic."

"Good for you. Well, happy hunting," Josie said, waving goodbye, then turning toward me. "Fifteen kids? Can you even imagine?"

"Not a chance," I said, shaking my head. "And that would have to be a lot harder than taking care of forty dogs, right?"

"No doubt about it," she said. "But one or two is starting to sound pretty good, isn't it?"

"Yeah, it is. But don't tell my mother I said that. She'll start trying to set me up on a daily basis. But the chances of it happening don't seem to be very good," I said.

"One step at a time," Josie deadpanned.

"What?"

"You might want to start by actually going out on a date."

"Look who's talking," I said, making a face at her. "I'd love to date, but I'm just not meeting anybody."

"Try to stop hanging around crime scenes," Josie said. "It's sort of a mood killer."

Chapter 14

I worked my way into the bathing suit my mother had given me for Christmas and reviewed the results in the mirror. The bare skin to fabric ratio was about ninety-nine to one, and the combination of the chocolate-brown suit, when set against the rosy pink hue that had yet to tan and the pale white patch of leg that would be making its first appearance in the sun in years, made the back of my upper thighs look like a carton of Neapolitan ice cream. But since my mother was already sitting by the pool with Chef Claire and Josie and would be watching me closely for the next several days to make sure I actually wore the thing, I did my best to tug and maneuver the swimsuit until I achieved maximum coverage. Since Henry, my mother's caretaker, was visiting friends on the other side of the island, I figured I was safe from him popping in for a chat and getting way too good of a look at me. I draped a towel over my shoulders, grabbed my sunglasses and a large bottle of sunscreen and headed for the pool. I paused in the doorway that led to the pool area, exhaled loudly, then walked outside.

"Wow," Josie deadpanned with a grin. "Nice buns. How do you manage to get them so white?"

"Shut it."

"Turn around and let me get a good look at you, darling."

I twirled a couple of times and felt my face redden.

"You look wonderful," my mother said, petting the King Charles that was perched on her lap. "But we do need to do a little work on the color matching. Your upper thigh looks like a tricolor flag at the moment. Of which country I'm not sure."

"Neapolistan," Josie said, grinning at me.

"Funny." I glared at her and wondered if three minutes was long enough to pay homage to a ridiculous Christmas present. I took a step toward the sliding glass doors that led back inside the house. "I'm going to go change."

"No, darling, don't," my mother said. "You look great."

"But it's so small," I said, glancing down at myself.

"It's Brazilian," my mother said. "They're all wearing them down there."

"Good for the Brazilians," I said, sitting down and beginning to slather myself with sunscreen.

As I rubbed the lotion into my skin, I watched the dogs in the pool tussling over a four-sided rope toy that had a rubber ball attached to each end. Captain was dominating and dragging the other dogs through the water at will, but Chloe and the two Goldens weren't going down without a fight. My mom's dogs, Summer and Winter, watched the action from their wet, cool perch on the top step of the pool. The water came up to their eyes, and their long, floppy ears seemed to be floating like water lilies.

"Any update on Rocco yet?" I said.

"I spoke with the police this morning," my mother said. "They wanted to arrest him, but they don't have enough at the moment. They're going to release him sometime around ten."

"That's good," I said. "The poor guy spends twenty years trying to put his past behind him, and then something like that happens."

"He'll be fine. And we all know Rocco didn't kill him," my mother said, adjusting her sunglasses as she stretched further out in her recliner. "Teresa called a little while ago and said they would be stopping by on their way home."

"Why do you think the guy got shot?" Chef Claire said as she sat up and pressed a finger into her chest to check for sunburn.

"He seemed to be a despicable human being," my mother said. "I'm not surprised at all."

"You're just mad because he called you a slimy carpetbagger," I said, laughing.

"Yeah," Josie said, laughing along. "That one had to hurt."

"And right in front of my friends," she said. "That was a cruel thing to say."

"Maybe you shot him, huh, Mom?"

"Me? You were the one who stabbed him, darling."

"Yeah, while trying to defend your honor," I said, glancing over at her as I struggled to apply sunscreen to my back.

"Oh, give me that," my mother said, reaching for the bottle of sunscreen. "Come here."

I sat down on the edge of her recliner, and she started rubbing the lotion on. She noticed my distant stare toward the beach.

"What is it, darling?"

"I just can't shake the idea that Gavin's murder is somehow linked to the woman we rescued from the water."

"Because that's all you've got at the moment?" Josie said.

"Pretty much," I said. "They were staying at the same guesthouse in town."

"As a couple?" my mother said.

"No, they had separate rooms," I said. "But that doesn't mean they weren't seeing each other. Geez, I wish he hadn't got shot. I really wanted to have a chat with him."

"I'm sure Gavin would feel the same way, darling," my mother said. "Now, stand up."

"I think I've got it from here, Mom."

"Don't be silly," she said. "I'm your mother. Trust me, I've had my hands on your tushie hundreds of times."

"Yeah, back when I was wearing footie PJs," I said, protesting.

"You ever had a sunburn there before?"

"No."

"Well, I don't recommend it," she said, her hands working on my upper thighs. "I fell asleep sunbathing several years ago and couldn't sit down for about three days. Nasty." She continued to rub lotion into my skin. "Darling?"

"Yeah?"

"You really need to get to the gym."

"Mom!"

"I'm not saying it's big. It could just use a little firming up. You're not getting any younger. And neither am I, as I'm forced to remind you on a regular basis."

I climbed back into my recliner and stretched out pouting. I put my sunglasses on and shook my head.

"Unbelievable. Does every conversation with you have to turn into your obsessive quest for grandkids?"

"Obsessive quest? That's a bit harsh, wouldn't you say?"

"What would you call it, Mom?"

"A wish? No, I'm gonna go with *dream*," she said, grinning as she glanced around at Josie and Chef Claire.

Before I had time to come up with a snappy comeback, we heard the sound of the outside gate opening. Rocco and Teresa waved as they strolled toward us and all six dogs spotted them immediately. They woofed and climbed out of the pool, then raced across the lawn toward our two guests. En masse, they stopped at their feet and shook, drenching them. Fortunately, both Rocco and Teresa were dog lovers and laughed as they resumed their approach.

"Sorry about that," I said.

"No problem," Rocco said. "After the night I just spent, I needed a shower."

"Are you guys okay?" I said, dragging a towel across my lap.

"The cops leaned on me pretty hard last night. And for very good reasons, Teresa is still pretty shaken up."

"The police had a field day with the idea that the current man in my life was responsible for getting rid of the former man in my life," Teresa said, shaking her head.

"But we'll be fine," Rocco said, squeezing Teresa's hand. "And don't worry Chef Claire, I'll be at the restaurant by five."

"Feel free to take the day off, Rocco," Chef Claire said. "In fact, take all time you need."

"What I need is to be at work," he said.

"Okay," she said, flashing him a warm smile. "It's your call."

"Are we interrupting anything?" Teresa said.

"No, we were just discussing...let's see," Josie deadpanned as she feigned deep thought. "I believe it was flags, grandchildren, and the importance of a regular toning regimen."

I did a slow burn in my recliner but stayed silent.

"You're not interrupting at all," my mother said, then glanced at me. "Isn't that right, darling?"

"Absolutely," I said, tight-lipped. "We're glad you stopped by. And we're more than ready for a new topic of conversation."

"And I was just about to head inside for a snack," Chef Claire said. "I know it's early, but I'm suddenly in the mood for some ice cream."

"That sounds great," Josie said, getting up from her recliner. "I'll give you a hand."

"Thanks."

"We got any Neapolitan?"

They both laughed, and it continued to drift out onto the patio long after they'd reached the kitchen.

Chapter 15

Later in the morning, after my mother and Rocco and Teresa left, it turned cloudy and cool, so I volunteered to take the dogs for a walk. I needed some time alone to sort through several thoughts and questions my neurons were having a field day with. I pulled on a pair of shorts and a tee shirt, grabbed a handful of tennis balls, and headed for the beach with the dogs bouncing at my feet woofing at me to stop hogging all the toys. I fired four balls in different directions and laughed as I watched the dogs try to decide which one had their name on it.

As we made our way down the beach and past my mother's house, it started to rain. It felt refreshing, and I was in no hurry to turn back. I continued my stroll along the edge of the water, occasionally bending down to pick up and throw a tennis ball whenever its current owner decided it was time for another sprint across the sand. I let my mind do its thing, and my thoughts eventually coalesced into a workable set of questions that wouldn't necessarily help me put the puzzle pieces together, but would at least give me a framework for organizing my thoughts and hopefully keep me from getting a headache in the process.

I focused at the beginning and turned my neurons loose.

What had the mystery woman and her King Charles been doing out in the middle of the ocean in a kayak in the dead of night?

Since Sylvia, the woman who ran the guesthouse, had told me that the woman named Bobbie, or Vera, or whatever the heck her name was, never went anywhere without her dog, I didn't worry about trying to connect that dot. All of us brought our dogs with us whenever possible, and it made perfect sense that the King Charles had been a welcome addition to the woman's kayak adventure.

I seriously doubted if being out on the water late at night had been planned. Paddling a kayak on the ocean in the middle of the day was enough to make my stress level redline. But being out there in complete darkness would turn me into a terror-stricken lunatic incapable of speech or rational thought. Any number of different kinds of shark could easily tip a fiberglass kayak, thereby adding a touch of salt to their food before enjoying their snack. And while the dwindling number of sharks in the waters around the islands continued to concern scientists and environmentalists, as Josie was always quick to point out whenever the subject came up, it only takes one.

No, I decided, being out on the water at night hadn't been the woman's plan.

I threw the tennis ball Chloe dropped at my feet and watched all four dogs race after it. Chloe lucked out with a good bounce and snatched it out of mid-air then taunted the others by inching close before dashing off. The rain began to pound, and when I reached Mr. Smith's former house, a magnificent property that seemed to rise right out of the sand, I turned around and whistled. The dogs, about a hundred yards away, saw me start walking toward home and tore after me. By the time they caught up, they were all panting and ready for a long drink and an extended nap. They each dropped their tennis ball, and I collected them and continued my slow stroll along the edge of the water. The rain poured off my head and face, but after a few days in the relentless hot sun and cloudless skies, I was in no hurry to get home. I refocused and let my neurons do their thing.

Why hadn't the mysterious woman made any effort to find her dog?

I'd been checking the local paper and various websites, as well as contacting all the vets and animal groups in the area, to see if anyone had reported a missing dog. But there was no mention of a King Charles Spaniel anywhere.

Perhaps the woman was unable to take care of the dog any longer and simply couldn't bear the thought of a tearful goodbye.

Perhaps she had been forced to go into hiding and was afraid to show her face around town for fear of being seen by her pursuers.

Perhaps she'd been abducted and was currently being held against her will, in a constant state of worry about her beloved Earl.

My neurons briefly flared when I landed on the abducted angle, but nothing held, and I moved on.

Perhaps the mysterious woman from the water had been the one who killed Teresa's ex-husband.

This idea held my attention, and I gave my brain some time to do its work. Since they knew each other from the guesthouse, maybe they had been a couple. Perhaps they'd had a fight, and she'd headed out with Earl for a kayak session to cool off. Or maybe they hadn't fought until they were out on the water in separate kayaks. And after the fight, Gavin had paddled back to shore and left her out there on her own. If the woman blamed Gavin for her recent brush with death, while it would have been an extreme overreaction, I supposed it was possible she'd been mad enough to shoot him.

But how would she have known he was in his car parked behind the restaurant?

Perhaps she had just happened to be walking by the restaurant when Rocco was wailing away at the man and seized the opportunity to take him out and get away unscathed. But why would the woman be walking around toting a twenty-two pistol? Then I considered the possibility that the gun had been in Gavin's car the whole time and the woman knew it. I slowed my stroll to a snail's pace and let that idea roll around in my head for several moments.

Then I felt the onset of a headache.

I brushed my soaked hair back from my face, checked to make sure the dogs were still nearby and picked up my pace to a slow lumber.

The idea of her carrying a gun could indicate she was either in danger or on a mission for revenge. And since I had no evidence of either, I let it go and focused on the gun itself. Two shots from a twenty-two in the back of the head was a well-known calling card of professional hit men working in organized crime. I pushed the thought that Rocco used to work in organized crime away for the moment and wondered what sort of activity Gavin might have been involved in that would raise the ire of people working in the underworld.

The possibility that the shooter had been at the restaurant the entire time surfaced, and I wracked my brain trying to remember some of the people who'd been sitting at various tables in the dining room. But my only solid memories were of a young couple who were on their honeymoon and extremely depressed by the painful sunburns they were both displaying, along with a tourist family of six that included four boisterous children and their mother and father who weren't speaking to each other. Other than that, I had no real memory of any other dinner guests except the people at our table. And I was certain that everyone at our table had been in their seats when we'd heard Teresa's scream.

By the time I finished kicking around the shooter-was-in-the-restaurant theory, I was getting close to home, and the dogs picked up their pace. I was also beginning to feel what I thought was chafing on my upper legs with every step. Then I realized that instead of chafing, what I was actually feeling was a sunburn. Apparently, even a sunscreen with an SPF high enough to block the gamma rays from a nuclear explosion wasn't enough to handle the intensity of the Caribbean sun, and I hoped I'd gotten out of the sun before I'd done any real damage.

I flinched with every step as the rain intensified, and what had started out as a leisurely stroll down an isolated stretch of sand had now turned into the last mile of a marathon. At least, I imagined it was what the last mile of a marathon would feel like: I didn't even like to *drive* twenty-six miles. But I trudged forward and noticed the dogs waiting for me about a hundred feet away with expectant looks on their faces.

"Yeah, I'm coming."

My neurons had performed well, but without any firm theories to hold onto, at the end of my stroll, I wasn't much further along than I'd been when I started. But I did come up with one trail that might be worth exploring. Since I was in Cayman, a place where high-finance and development deals seemed to rule, I decided that I might have a chat with Gerald, the Finance Minister. If there was a project going on in the islands that might have provoked someone to murder a hanger-on like Gavin, Gerald would know about it. And while he might have no inclination to tell me about it, I figured my Snoopmeter along with its built-in lie detector might be enough to get me on the right track.

And if Gavin's murder and the disappearance of the mystery woman were somehow connected, I might be able to work backwards from whatever development deal was in the works, uncover who parked two, twenty-twos in the back of Gavin's head, and, from there, possibly track down the woman and give her back her dog. That is if I could pry Earl from my mother's lap, the place where the King Charles appeared to have taken up permanent residence.

It certainly wasn't an elegant strategy, and I knew that I'd probably end up annoying countless people in the process. But I'd learned that situations like these were more of an art form than science, and I was pretty sure this one wasn't laid out like an Escher; mathematically-inspired works of art, multi-medium enigmas that, despite their amazing ability to surprise and delight and make you wonder if your eyes were playing tricks on you, eventually wound back on themselves in perfect symmetry.

No, by the time this one was over, I was pretty sure it would resemble something from the abstract expressionist catalog.

Move over, Mr. Pollock. Here I come again.

I left the water's edge and slowly slogged through the deeper sand that was now wet and tugging at my calves. I groaned and grimaced with every step, and the dogs continued to trot in small circles impatiently urging me to get it into gear. Apparently tired of waiting, Captain woofed his displeasure.

"I said, I'm coming."

I left the beach and took several gulps of cool air then trudged up the small incline that led to the gate. At the top of the incline, I paused to catch my breath and turned around to watch the raindrops relentlessly pound the ocean surface. It would be a bad time to be out on the ocean, particularly in something as small and vulnerable as a kayak.

What the heck was she doing out there at night?

Where on earth had she gone?

And who the heck is Owen?

I opened the gate, and the dogs raced toward Chef Claire and Josie who were sitting under the patio awning, completely dry. At least they were until the dogs arrived. I slowly made my way across the lawn and headed for a recliner next to them. I sat down gingerly and winced. Josie stared at me, then shook her head and tossed me a towel.

"Let me guess, that look is from your early sea otter period, right?"

"Funny. Actually, the rain felt great."

"I'll take your word for it," Chef Claire said, doing her best to fend off Al and Dente who seemed to think it had been a month since they'd seen their mama. "Yuk. Which one of you smells like dead fish?"

"I think it's Al," I said, "I'm sorry about that. But he started rolling around in something way down the beach before I could stop him."

"Then he's just going to have to stay outside until he gets a bath, aren't you?"

Al didn't like the sound of that and made it a point to rub himself all over her.

"I couldn't help but notice you've got a little hitch in your giddy-up there, Hopalong," Josie said, raising an eyebrow. "Did you pull something?"

"No. Butt burn," I said, shifting uncomfortably.

"Ouch," Josie said, frowning. "I guess we'll just have dinner at the bar, and you can eat standing up."

"Good plan."

"Did you make any progress?"

"No, I thought I'd just start by asking Gerald a bunch of questions about what sort of projects are in the works at the moment and see if that leads me anywhere."

"Ah, the annoyance factor. An oldie but a goodie."

"You gotta play to your strengths, right?"

"Maybe he'll feel sorry for you and open up," Josie deadpanned.

"What?"

"Show him your sunburn. That should do the trick."

Chapter 16

The Government Administration Building, home to the majority of departments responsible for keeping things running smoothly, is a six-story office building in downtown Georgetown that reminds me of a high-school or a hospital. I was escorted to the fifth floor and then into a large, plush office that definitely delivered when it came to sending the intended message: The person who works here is important and has some serious juice.

"He'll be right with you," my escort said, then she pointed at two leather chairs framing a coffee table. "Please, have a seat."

"Maybe in a minute," I said, not relishing the thought.

I still couldn't believe how bad a sunburn I'd gotten yesterday. Three hours in the mid-morning sun and my backside had turned a shade of pink that reminded me of a medium-rare steak, minus the grill marks. This morning, I'd taken a cold shower then slathered myself in a pineapple-scented Aloe Vera lotion that definitely helped. But I was now exuding a scent that had Chef Claire and Josie, in the manner of a Pavlovian-dog conditioned to respond to various stimuli, reaching into the fridge for the fruit salad. I'd opted for the loosest fitting pair of shorts and blouse I could find to minimize the amount of contact the soft cotton would have with my skin, then gingerly settled in behind the wheel of the jeep and made the drive without tearing up once.

In short, I was pretty sure my sunburn was now bearable.

That is, as long as I didn't move or breathe too hard.

Like other executives with big offices and a lot of wall space to cover, Gerald was fond of pictures of himself posing with a wide variety of people. I recognized several celebrities, a couple of athletes, and some U.S. government officials who looked vaguely familiar. Gerald looked pretty much the same in all the photos; an enormous smile, arm around the shoulder, or the lower back when posing with women, and a twinkle in his eyes that left no doubt he was most definitely living and enjoying the good life.

I half-turned when he entered the office through a different door and beamed at me. He was wearing a soft-gray suit with a white shirt and lavender tie and looked fantastic. It was the first time I'd ever seen him wearing anything other than shorts and a colorful short-sleeved shirt, and it caught me by surprise. He'd suddenly transitioned into someone who was a lot more than just my mother's good friend. Now, he was a guy who worked in the inner circle of the power structure and was a major player in pretty much everything that happened down here.

My neurons had been correct. He was definitely the right guy to start my search with. But I suddenly felt tentative. Either it was the trappings of the office or the way he was dressed, but I heard my subconscious telling me to tread carefully. This wasn't a casual barbecue sitting around my mom's pool sipping Mudslides. This place was all business, and I knew instinctively how I needed to conduct myself. Professional. Prim and proper. A woman of substance who demonstrated the requisite amount of respect for the office and the man, but someone still worthy of being treated as an equal.

Pleased with my planned approach, I nodded to myself then felt my sunburn begin to itch. Knowing that scratching my butt in the middle of the Finance Minister's office probably wouldn't help me convey the image I was trying to project, I tried to ignore the itch. Then I realized Gerald was talking to me.

"What?" I said, fighting the urge to imitate Chloe and rub myself vigorously against the wall.

"I said, are you all right?" he said, laughing. "You seemed to be off in another world."

"Oh, that," I said. "Don't worry about that. It happens all the time. I was just looking at all your photos and got carried away. You know a lot of very important people."

"Ah," he said, waving it off. "Occupational hazard. How are you?"

"Apart from dealing with a rather nasty sunburn, I'm good. Thanks for taking the time to see me."

"My pleasure," he said, his eyes twinkling. "Yes, I heard about your burn. That's too bad. They can be most unpleasant."

"You heard?" I said, frowning. "You talked to my mother, didn't you?"

"Sure. I talk with her pretty much every day," he said, then sniffed the air. "I smell pineapple."

"Yeah, that's me. Sorry. I think I used a bit too much lotion."

"That's understandable," he said, sympathetically. "I used to try all sorts of things whenever I got a bad sunburn."

"You don't get burned anymore?" I said, surprised.

"Not really," he said, shaking his head.

"Because you're dark-skinned, right?"

"No," he said, staring at me like I'd lost my mind. "I don't burn because I try to stay out of the sun."

"Sure, sure," I said, my face turning as red as my bottom. "I'm sorry. I didn't mean to…"

"Don't worry about it," he said, laughing. "But trust me, people with my skin color sunburn just like everyone else."

Way to go, Suzy. So much for staying professional. And we were already looking at prim and proper in the rearview mirror. I smelled like a Hawaiian fruit plantation, had made an unintentional reference to his skin color that he could have easily categorized as racist, and I was doing everything I could not to rub myself against the furniture to ease the itch my neurons were screaming at me to scratch.

Smooth.

"Would you care to sit down?" he said, still beaming at me.

"If I have to," I said, inching my way toward one of the leather chairs and gingerly sitting down. The chair provided enough relief from the itch to outweigh the pain, and I gently wiggled back and forth on the soft leather. "Okay, that's not too bad."

"I have to say, Suzy, that you are truly a unique individual," he said, sitting down across from me and grinning at my attempt to get comfortable.

"Yeah, I get that a lot," I said, sighing with pleasure as the itch finally subsided.

"You mentioned over the phone that you'd like to discuss a development deal of some sort?" he said, draping a leg over his knee, suddenly all business.

"Yes, I would."

"Don't tell me that you'd like to invest some of your considerable resources in a project? Perhaps, some commercial real estate. Or maybe you'd like to get a piece of a planned community. I have several possibilities I've been trying to get your mother interested in."

"No, I'm not looking to invest," I said, allowing myself another wiggle. "I'm trying to reunite a dog with his owner."

He blinked but did his best not to reveal what he was thinking. Which I'm sure was who is this crazy woman sitting in my office.

"I see," he said eventually with a frown. "I'm not sure I can make the connection."

"Yeah, me either," I said, making the mistake of leaning forward in my chair. I flinched, took a few moments to wait out the pain, then continued. "At the moment, I only have a working theory."

"Your mother calls them wild-eyed guesses," he said, laughing.

"Tomato, tomahto," I said, shrugging. "My theory is that Gavin, the guy who got shot at the restaurant, and the woman I'm trying to track down might have been working together."

"The woman you're trying to find so you can return her dog?" he said.

"Yes. And I don't have a clue where or how to find her. But since Gavin worked in real estate development, I thought if I could identify some of the current projects that are going on down here, I might be able to work backward from there and track the woman down."

"And figure out who shot Gavin in the process, right?" he said, grinning at me with a raised eyebrow.

"Well, yeah, there is that," I said, grinning back.

"The police seem to think that your friend Rocco killed him."

"No," I said, firmly shaking my head. "Rocco didn't do it."

"Based on what I've seen of his prior record, a rather *colorful* history I'm sure you'd agree, he seems to be a likely suspect."

"No, he's moved way past his former life," I said, then stopped and stared at him. "Based on what you've seen?"

"Yes, I reviewed his file just this morning," he said, nodding.

"Why would you do that?" I said, frowning.

"Suzy, I'm the Finance Minister, and all of us in the government take murder very seriously. It tends to make the tourists nervous. Besides, like you, I can be a bit nosy."

"Okay, I get that," I said. "But if you were reading the case file you would have also seen that he wasn't anywhere near the parking lot behind the restaurant. He was working behind the bar. And you were there the whole time."

"Yes, I was," he said. "And I saw him use Gavin's head to open the front door. By his own admission, Rocco was the one who drove the car and parked it behind the restaurant."

"But that was earlier," I said, shaking my head.

"The approximate time of death fits into the timeframe when he was in the car with Gavin," he said softly.

"No, Rocco didn't do it," I said. "It didn't happen."

"Let's just let the police do their thing and let it play out, okay?"

"Is that your way of telling me to mind my own business, Gerald?"

"Let's call it a suggestion, shall we?"

"Sure, sure," I said, nodding. "But two in the back of the head wouldn't be the way Rocco would have done it."

"Tenacious, aren't we?" he said, running a hand through his hair. "Given Rocco's former employer, I would think that might be exactly the way he would have done it."

"No, his time working for the mob is ancient history. And Rocco's problems with Gavin were more of a personal nature. If Rocco was going to take him out, he wouldn't have passed up the chance to see the look on Gavin's face when he did it."

"Personal, you say. Do tell."

I'd walked right into that one.

I wiggled in my chair and felt the leather brushing against my bare skin. Confused, but determined to get out of the hole I might have just dug for Rocco, I ignored the fact that my blouse must be riding up my back and continued.

"Yes, Gavin had been stalking his ex-wife. Teresa, remember?"

"The woman who is running your new animal shelter," he said.

"Yes. And she and Rocco are in love," I said. "Rocco didn't want her feeling threatened or afraid."

"You're really not helping his case, Suzy," Gerald said, shaking his head.

"Rocco didn't do it, Gerald," I said firmly. "But since you raise the possibility of organized crime, are they active down here?"

"Given our banking system, any group like theirs with that much money is most definitely active," he said, shrugging. "But they most certainly are not involved with any government-sponsored or approved development projects. And from what I've seen of their operation, I think *organized* might be a bit of an overstatement."

"But there must be lots of other projects going on that the government isn't involved with, right?"

"Of course," he said, "But we do our best to keep a close eye on everything that's going on around the islands."

"So it's possible they might be involved in a deal that might not, shall we say, pass the government smell test?"

"If I've learned anything in my career, it's that anything is possible," he said, shrugging. "Especially when large sums of money are involved."

"Have you heard about any suspicious projects?" I said, leaning forward and again feeling the touch of soft leather against my back. I tugged my blouse down and wiggled gently. Flash of pain, nagging itch. "You know, any projects that seem a bit *off-key?*"

"Off-key?" he said, laughing. "Like a community musical theatre group?"

"Funny."

"Sure, I hear rumors all the time."

"And?"

"And if I spent time trying to track them all down, I would never do anything else. You might find it hard to believe, but I have a pretty big job."

He sat back in his chair and studied me closely.

"I know you think that I'm some sort of corrupt public official, but, over time, you'll come to understand that things simply work a bit differently down here than you're used to back home."

"I never said you were corrupt, Gerald," I said, frowning at him. "I just think you're a little loosey-goosey with the rules."

"Loosey-goosey? Is that a technical term?" he said, grinning at me.

"Hey, whatever works, right?" I said, relaxing as I remembered just how much I liked the man. "You don't know of any projects like that?"

"No, I'm afraid not," he said, shaking his head.

"Any ideas where I might look?"

"Geez, Suzy, I wish I could be more help," he said. "But if you're going to keep digging, and I'm sure you are, about the only idea I might have would be for you to look into recent or pending sales of vacant land. Knowing Gavin like I did, whatever he was working on was probably being funded by dirty money. And a great place to hide money down here is to put it in businesses that cater to tourists. And if a project like that created a lot of jobs, our government might be willing to be a bit *flexible* when it comes to the source of the money. That is, as long as the people funding the deal didn't try to embarrass us by being blatant or trying to rub our face in it."

"Like a big hotel or resort?" I said.

"Always a popular choice," he said, nodding. "But there's nothing on my radar at the moment."

"But it's possible that there's something out there that's still in the planning stage and hasn't hit your desk yet?"

"Absolutely," he said. "That happens quite often. Unfortunately, some people think they can get away with all sorts of things without us knowing about it. But we always find out at some point."

"That's why you're not worried about the possibility of something nefarious going on at the moment?"

"Pretty much," he said, nodding as he glanced at his watch. "Look, as much as I'd like to sit here and watch you wiggle, I have a meeting that is about to start."

"Of course," I said. "Thanks again for meeting with me. Will we see you at the restaurant soon?"

"Actually, your mother has invited me to join her tonight," he said, standing up.

"Great. We'll see you then."

Then something happened I was sure would haunt me for years to come. I got up out of my chair and realized, too late, that what I thought had been my blouse creeping up my back was actually my baggy shorts falling down. When I stood, my shorts fell around my ankles, and my feet caught in them when I frantically bent down to pull them up. I fell forward on the floor face down right in front of Gerald just as the woman who had escorted me into the office earlier knocked softly on the door then opened it.

"Gerald, your meeting is about to start," she said, then caught a glimpse of me sprawled on the floor at her boss's feet. "Oh, Gerald. Really? For God's sake, not in your office."

"Suzy was just showing me her sunburn," Gerald said, embarrassed but unable to stop laughing.

"Of course, she was," she said, shaking her head as she backed out of the office. "I'll tell them you're on your way."

I climbed to my feet and pulled my shorts up and tucked the blouse in.

"I can't believe it," I said, my face burning hot with embarrassment.

"Don't worry about it," he said, wiping his eyes.

"You can stop laughing now, Gerald," I snapped.

"That really is a nasty burn," he said, then burst into another round of laughter.

He gestured toward the door, and I rapidly headed for it, desperate to get out of the building before the story of my showing the goods to the Finance Minister went viral around the office.

"If I may offer an observation," Gerald said, finally getting his laughter under control.

"I really wish you wouldn't, Gerald."

"Fair enough," he said, grinning at me. "But if I were to do so, the word I would use would be *outstanding*."

"How about we just forget the whole thing, okay?"

"Oh, I seriously doubt if I'm going to be able to do that."

I headed out of the office, down the hall to the elevator, and then out the building just as fast my little sunburned body would allow.

Chapter 17

I stood tall at the bar as I cut a piece of steak and raised the fork to my mouth. After swallowing, I took a sip of water and leaned forward with my elbows on the bar. Josie, sitting next to me, took a big bite of fish and studied me closely as she chewed.

"And that was when you decided to flash Gerald?"

"No, that came later," I said, shaking my head. "And for the tenth time, it wasn't a conscious choice. It was an accident."

"We'll get back to that later," she said, grinning. "Did he have anything to say that might be useful?"

"Not really."

"Because he was too busy ogling, right?"

I flinched as I reached for my glass of wine but recovered quickly. "He said he didn't know anything specific going on at the moment that Gavin might have been involved in. But I still don't know if I can believe a word Gerald says."

"Because he called your butt outstanding, right?"

"Will you please stop? I'm embarrassed enough as it is already. I can't imagine what they're saying around that office."

"Oh, I can," Josie said, grinning as she slid another piece of fish into her mouth. "And after you found yourself on all fours in Gerald's office, you were too embarrassed to come home?"

"No."

"Then where were you all day?"

"I was doing some research. Land deals, pending property sales, stuff like that," I said, stabbing a mushroom with my fork. "These are fantastic."

"They are," she said, spearing one off my plate. "Did you find anything out?"

"Not really," I said. "I just can't make much sense of who all the players are. I spent a lot of time reviewing the list of registered companies down here."

"And all you found was the usual spider web of different companies layered on top of each other until it's impossible to understand who owns what."

"Nothing gets past you," I said, nodding.

"It's nice of you to notice," she said, stabbing another of my mushrooms.

"Then I spent a couple of hours reading some articles and government reports about the ongoing battle between the developers and the conservationists. It looks like there's a lot of pressure on the government to start setting aside some areas as protected. They're even talking about a national park."

"Okay, that's interesting. I can see why some of the development companies might not be happy about that possibility," she said, nodding. "Keep going."

"It wasn't clear who they are, and there weren't a lot of direct references, but it looks like there's somebody down here who might be trying to buy up parcels of land that are part of the areas that might end up protected. Or protected-adjacent."

"Protected-adjacent? Did you come up with that one all by yourself?"

"Yeah," I said, glancing at her. "Not bad, huh?"

"Companies trying to buy up everything they can get their hands on are hardly a mystery, Suzy," Josie said, reaching for her wine and taking a sip. "They're all over the place."

"Yeah, I know. But who would go to all that effort to buy up a bunch of property that's about to be protected by the government? It's not like you can build a bunch of McMansions on a national park."

"Shhh, don't give them any ideas," Josie said, shaking her head and laughing. "For sale, an eight-bedroom chalet complete with wine cellar and a view overlooking Mount Rushmore."

I laughed along then took another bite of my steak.

"Did you come up with any names yet?" Josie said.

"There were a lot of names mentioned in the articles. But they were inconsistent. One company mentioned as a potential buyer in one article would be identified as the seller in the next. And it was impossible to follow the thread."

"Maybe that's the way some people like it," Josie said, pushing her plate away and reaching for the dessert menu. "Maybe they think it's really not anybody's business."

"Yeah, I'm sure you're right. I was just about to give up, then I found an obscure article that came the closest to laying out the story. But even that one wasn't clear. At one point, the journalist just started asking a bunch of questions in the middle of the article. You know, why would so and so do that? Who is the mysterious company behind all this? Why won't they show their face? What do they have to hide?"

"Questions a reporter might actually get answered before they wrote the story, right?" she said.

"Yeah, that was my first thought, too. It seemed like sort of a fishing expedition. So I reread it. And it comes across as a piece that was written almost like a dare. Like the journalist was taunting somebody to show their face and make themselves known. The tone was very anti-development."

"Left-wing?"

"Pretty much," I said, finishing my wine and waving at Rocco for two more.

"Who wrote the article?"

"That's the weird part," I said, leaning closer to scan the dessert menu she was holding. "There wasn't a name on it. All it had was the name of the paper the article was published in. It's some local freebie that includes all sorts of stuff for sale and discount offers and giveaways for local businesses. You know, like the Pennysaver. But with a major left-wing slant."

"The Commie Coupon Clipper?" Josie said, laughing.

"Yeah, that's pretty close," I said, nodding. "And the paper definitely has a conservation and environmental theme to it."

"Well, that explains the anti-development tone of the article, right?"

"Yes, it does. And I think I have an idea," I said.

"You're going to go to their office and buy an ad for a special deal here at the restaurant, aren't you?" she said, raising an eyebrow at me.

"You are on fire today," I said, gently punching her on the shoulder.

"Well, since I'm sitting next to you, it's a little hard not to be," she deadpanned. "You're throwing off some serious heat."

"Funny," I said, glancing around to make sure no one was watching before I gently scratched my sunburn. "Since I've got nothing else to go on, I thought it was worth a shot."

"You've had worse ideas."

"Yeah, I certainly have," I said, placing my elbows back on the bar. "The whole thing is really strange, and it's just a jumble of disconnected bits of information. And several names keep coming up in a lot of the articles, but there's nothing about who they are, or who works for them. But there was one name that caught my eye. And it wasn't clear if it's the name of a company or a person."

"What's the name?"

"Jansmid."

Josie frowned as she searched her memory bank, then shook her head.

"No, I got nothing."

"I couldn't find anything online. No website. No references to anybody that seemed relevant."

"Maybe it's a new company."

"But wouldn't that be all the more reason for them to be getting the word out?" I said.

"One would think," Josie said, glancing at the front door. "But here comes Gerald. Why don't you ask him?"

"That's my plan," I said, waving to him and my mother as they approached.

"Just try to keep your pants on."

"It's going to take me years to live this one down, isn't it?"

"At least," Josie said, laughing. "Hi, folks. How are you this lovely evening?"

"Wonderful, Josie," my mother said, leaning in for a quick hug and a kiss. "Hello, darling." She gave me a hug and then stared at me with a mischievous grin plastered on her face. "How was your day?"

"You know perfectly well how my day was, Mom," I said, glaring at her. "Hello, Gerald."

"Hi, Suzy," he said, his eyes twinkling. "I'm so sorry about what happened this morning."

"I'm sure it caused quite a stir around the office," I said, feeling my face start to flush red.

"Indeed," he said, nodding. "Everyone is dying to know who the mysterious naked woman is."

"I wasn't naked," I snapped. "I was just…severely under clothed."

Josie and my mother snorted loudly. I ignored them and motioned for Gerald to follow me. I took a few steps away from the bar, and when we were safely out of earshot, I continued.

"After I left your office, I did a little digging into a few things."

"I'd be shocked if you hadn't," he said, nodding. "What did you find out?"

"Not a lot," I said. "But have you ever heard of a company or an individual with the name Jansmid?"

He flinched, then recovered and nodded.

"Yes, I have," Gerald said. "And it's a name that many of us are trying to track down."

"You don't know who it is?"

"No, I don't," he said. "You must have read the article in that left-wing rag."

"I did. How did you know that?"

"Because that's the only place I've ever seen it mentioned," he said. "But we are definitely most interested in finding out who they are."

"Because they might be in the process of trying to buy up a bunch of land that could end up on the protected list, right?"

"You have been busy," he said. "I'm impressed. It took my staff a week to put that together."

"I couldn't find the name mentioned anywhere in the corporate registry," I said.

"And you won't," he said, shaking his head. "We've scoured our database, and it's simply not there."

"That must mean this Jansmid is an individual, right?"

"We are certainly looking into that possibility," he said.

"So Jansmid is definitely on the government's radar."

"It's one of those rumors we discussed earlier today," Gerald said.

"But you said you usually ignore all of them," I said.

"I did say that, didn't I?"

"Yes, but you're taking this one seriously?"

"We are," he said, nodding. "Relations between our developers and the residents are a bit strained at the moment. And the last thing we want is somebody driving a wedge further between them. Some of the tension is being driven by groups opposed to what they consider unchecked development. It's a situation that needs to be carefully managed."

"I see," I said, trying to process his comment. "And you're looking for a way to find the right *balance* between the two?"

"I am," he said, grinning at me. "I like to call it *pragmatic protection* of the environment."

"How very corporate of you," I said, flashing him a coy smile.

"Hey, I enjoy looking at fish and birds as much as the next guy, but I have responsibilities to help make sure the economy keeps ticking along."

"Do you ever stop to think about what you're going to do when you run out of land to build on?" I said.

"Oh, I'm sure I'll be out of office long before that happens," he said, turning around to accept the glass of wine my mother was offering. "Thanks."

"What are you talking about, darling?" she said, touching glasses with him then taking a sip of wine.

"At the moment, Gerald's insatiable need to cover every stretch of sand with concrete," I said, shaking my head at him.

"I was joking, Suzy," he said, then turned to my mother. "Does she get that annoying trait from you?"

"I'm going to need you to be a bit more specific, Gerald," she said, giving me a coy smile. "Which annoying trait are you referring to?"

"Funny, Mom," I said, getting testy. "I'm just trying to understand a few things so I can track down Earl's owner."

"Earl is doing just fine, darling," she said. "His eye has returned to normal, and he spent all day playing with Summer and Winter. And they're getting along so well."

"We need to find his owner, Mom. I know you've gotten attached to him, but you'd be devastated if either of your dogs got separated from you."

"Of course," she said, turning serious. "You're absolutely right. But I've grown very fond of the little guy."

"Well, if we don't find the owner soon, you might end up having to keep him."

"I could live with that," she said, then glanced at the front door. "Oh, there's John."

I watched John Smith as he paused in the doorway, glanced around, then spotted Gerald and my mother and waved. He casually strolled our way, then shook hands with all three of us, and looked around the full dining room.

"Busy," he said, nodding. "I guess the word is already out about how good the food is here."

"Yes, we're pretty happy so far," I said. "How are you, John?"

"I'm good," he said without giving it much thought. "Are we ready to eat? I'm starving." He took another look around the restaurant shuffling his feet, apparently anxious to sit down.

"You're in a hurry," Gerald said, laughing.

"Like I say, I'm starving," John Smith said, casting a loving stare at a tray of entrees one of the servers passed by carrying.

"Keep your pants on," Gerald said, shaking his head.

Then he caught himself and glanced back and forth at my mother and me. A wicked grin appeared on my mother's face, and she glanced over at me.

"Not a word, Mom."

Chapter 18

The office of *The People's Paradise* was a multicolored, nondescript, single story structure that appeared to be a house that had been converted into office space. It sat on the edge of town and had either managed to fend off redevelopment efforts or had yet to hit the radar of people who I was sure would love nothing more than raze it with a bulldozer and start over. But it had sort of a cool, funky vibe that I liked, and I parked in front then headed inside. What I was sure used to be the living room had been converted into a workspace, and four desks were positioned around the room in a manner that provided the most privacy for each occupant. But given the small amount of square footage, I doubted if the location of the desks made much of a difference. Three of the desks were unoccupied, but a woman sat at the other one that faced the front door. She looked up when I entered, removed her glasses, and beamed at me as she gestured for me to come closer.

"Welcome to The People's Paradise," she said. "Please have a seat. I just need to finish this up. I'll be right with you."

I sat down across from her and looked around the room. It was painted a bright red, the preferred color of communists everywhere, and a diverse collection of posters of famous revolutionaries inscribed with pithy quotes about the common good and struggles of the working class adorned the walls. Marx, Lenin, Trotsky, Fidel, and Che were all well-represented, and my capitalist instincts raised their ugly head when I caught myself wondering if their various estates were receiving royalties.

Then I caught a strong whiff of the dominant odor pervading the room. *Eau de Frat House* was what came to mind, and I picked up the scent of fruit, rum, stale beer, sweat, and weed. Then I noticed a couple of broken lamps and chairs that had been tossed haphazardly into a corner of the room. If this place was indeed considered paradise for those on the far left of the political spectrum, I think I'll keep dancing with the one that brought me, our present state of affairs notwithstanding.

The woman must have noticed my reaction, even though she hadn't looked up from her computer screen. "Staff party," she said, tapping the keyboard. "We have one each week after the new issue is put to bed." She glanced up briefly. "Last night was a particularly good one." Then she went back to her typing. "We have quite an interesting mix of people working here, and sometimes the conversations tend to get pretty heated."

"I guess your brand of politics attracts a wide range of different people, right?"

"Politics doesn't make strange bedfellows, marriage does," she said, finally making eye contact. "One of Marx's better quotes, don't you think?"

"Karl Marx said that?" I said, frowning.

"No, Groucho," she said, grinning. "They hate when I joke about their political views."

"So, you don't consider yourself one of the downtrodden proletariat?"

"Usually only on Monday mornings," she said, shrugging as she reached for her cup of coffee. "I work on commission and have a mortgage to pay. As such, my politics are more grounded in reality. How can I help you?"

"I'd like to place an ad for our restaurant," I said, pulling out the mockup Josie and Chef Claire had helped me come up with over breakfast. I handed it to her. "We're starting a two for one special on Tuesday nights."

"Okay," she said, scanning the mockup. "What size ad would you like to run?"

She handed me a laminated pricing sheet that outlined the various sizes and prices of each option. I studied it, decided on a quarter-page ad that would run for the next three weeks, then slid a credit card across the desk. As she processed the payment, I took another look around the otherwise empty room.

"I read a very interesting article in one of your recent issues," I said, casually.

"Really?" she said, sounding surprised. "Which one?"

"It was focused on the battle between the developers and environmentalists over what should and shouldn't be protected land."

"I remember that one," she said, sliding the credit card back to me. "It raised some interesting points, but I had a hard time following the thread."

"Yeah, me too," I said. "Do you know who wrote it?"

"Apparently, it was some guest columnist that Frederick crossed paths with. I never met the person who wrote it."

"Frederick?"

"Our publisher," she said, nodding her head toward the doorway behind her. "He's the leader of this intrepid little band of 21st century revolutionaries. His term, not mine."

"Are there others like you working here?" I said. "You know, other capitalists who like having a little walking-around money?"

"Well, there's Frederick. And there's one other person who sells ads, but I haven't seen him in three days," she said, shrugging. "I think he might have quit."

"That must make it hard on you," I said, sneaking a peek past her desk at the doorway.

"Not really," she said, shaking her head. "More money for me. And the rest of the staff pretty much leaves me alone since I'm the only one generating any revenue that keeps the place running."

"I see," I said, frowning. "What do the other people do?"

"Talk and argue mostly," she said, sliding my receipt across the desk. "Just sign the top copy, please. And when they're not arguing, they're usually drinking and smoking weed."

"Nice work if you can get it, huh?" I signed the receipt and slid her copy back.

"I don't mind," she said. "As long as they don't interfere with my ability to make a living, I don't care if they spend all day sitting in a tree."

"Is Frederick around today?"

"Yes, he's back there."

"Do you think it would be possible for me to have a quick word with him about the article?"

"I don't see why not," she said, standing up. "I'm sure he can tear himself away from the worker's struggle for a few minutes." Then she chortled, obviously delighted with her joke.

I sat quietly and checked my phone for messages while I waited. A few minutes later, she returned and gestured for me to follow her.

"Down the hall on your right. Just stay out of arms reach, and you'll be fine," she said, handing me one of her business cards. "And thanks for the business. I hope the ad works for you. If you want to run more, just stop by or give me a call."

I entered the large, plush office that contained an ensuite, and I assumed it used to be the master bedroom. The man behind the desk had his back to me and was intensely focused on the video game he was playing. He had streaks of gray in his ponytail and was wearing a faded tee shirt and beach shorts.

"Have a seat," he said, thumbs a blur and not looking up from the imperialist army he was doing battle with. "Want a cookie? They're *really* good." He paused long enough to nod at the plate of chocolate chip cookies next to him.

"Thanks," I said, starting to reach for one before pausing when my neurons fired urging caution. "What makes them so good?"

"Oh, just a special ingredient," he said, giggling. "Dang it. I never saw the little bugger coming." He tossed the handheld game console away in disgust and swiveled around in his chair. "Whoa. Jessie didn't mention how hot you were."

"Good for Jessie," I said, her comment about keeping my distance now making sense.

"Who are you?" he said, extending the plate of chocolate chip cookies that looked delicious.

"I'm Suzy Chandler," I said, staring despondently at the plate. "There's weed in the cookies, isn't there?"

"Sure," he said, nodding. "I find the symmetry of eating something that continues to make you hungry the more you eat fascinating."

"Sure, sure. Sort of a circle of life thing, right?"

He frowned, considered the idea, then gave me a bobblehead doll nod.

"Good analogy. Try one."

"I think I'll pass. Thanks," I said, sitting down without being invited. If it offended him, he didn't show it. But he was so stoned, he might not have even noticed I'd sat down.

"Jessie mentioned you wanted to discuss a recent article. The one about the protected land movement, right?"

"That's the one," I said, draping a leg across my knee and realizing that my sunburn was starting to abate. "I just have a few questions about it."

"Don't we all," he said, laughing and shaking his head. "I tried to read it after smoking this huge blunt and got completely lost. All those different scenarios and company names. After I'd reread the first paragraph four times, I gave up." He moved his hand over the top of his head as if it were a plane taking off. "You know, it went way over my head."

"Got it. So, you didn't work on the article?" I said.

"Me? Oh, no way," he said, shaking his head again as he reached for another cookie. "Are you sure? They're really good."

"No, thanks. I never cookie and drive."

He stared at me, trying to make sense of my comment, but decided clarification probably wasn't worth the effort. He draped a leg over his knee, revealing a very expensive style of shoe.

"I'm hoping I might be able to speak with the person who wrote the article," I said, leaning my head to one side to catch his eyes that were drifting around the office.

"I can't help you with that," he said, eventually. "I'm not sure where she is."

"She? So it's a woman?"

"Yeah. Abigail," he said, nodding. "She had an accident on Christmas Day, and nobody has seen her since."

Lightbulbs started popping in my head, and I forced myself to remain calm.

"What's her last name?

"No idea," he said, shrugging. "I'm surprised I remembered Abigail. We only met a couple of times."

"What sort of accident did she have?" I said, casually.

"Apparently, she almost drowned and had to be rescued. I heard about it and went to the hospital to see how she was doing, but she'd already been discharged. And nobody has seen her around since then. Her taking off like that has left a big hole in the paper. We were planning on doing a four-part series." He drifted off and started talking to the wall. "I guess I'll just have to dig up a few classic manifestos out of the archives. We'll call it... a *retrospective collection*. Yeah, that'll work." Then he turned back to me and flinched, apparently surprised to see me still sitting there. He flashed me a small grin. "I said that out loud, didn't I?"

I flashed him a grin and nodded. He grabbed another cookie and stared lovingly at the game console.

"You don't have any idea where she might be?"

"Not a clue," he said, shrugging. "Like I said, I barely knew her, and she seems to be a very private person."

"But she shares your political views?"

"When it comes to the environment," he said, taking a bite of cookie. "But when it comes to money, she's pseudo-proletariat. I'm pretty sure she comes from big money and doesn't seem to mind if people know it."

"Just like you, right?" I said, deciding to test out one of the theories my neurons had been nagging me about since I'd sat down.

"What?" he said, stuffing the rest of a half-eaten cookie in his mouth.

I swallowed hard. They did look like some very tasty cookies.

"You also seem to be a man of considerable means," I said. "That's a top of the line computer, your taste in art is impeccable, and those Mauri ostrich sneakers you're wearing go for nine hundred a pair."

"What are you, some sort of lifestyle consultant? Maybe a fashion expert?" he said, dropping his leg from his knee and sliding his feet under the desk.

"No, but my mother is determined to teach me everything she knows," I said, shrugging. "You come from money, don't you?"

"Not that it's any of your business, but as a matter of fact I do," he said, rediscovering a bit of focus.

"Are you a local?"

"Pretty much. We moved here when I was very young. But I try to get away a few times a year. I like to ski."

"Ah, Aspen and the Swiss Alps," I said, giving him a knowing smile. "Not places I would choose to assuage the guilt that comes with being a man of means. But whatever works, huh?"

"Do you come from money?" he said, studying me closely.

"Yeah, I do."

"Then you know what it's like to be able to do anything you want while millions of people are starving. How do you deal with it?"

"I spend as much of mine as I can on dogs," I said.

"Dogs? Yeah, I can see that working," he said, giving it some serious consideration. "I sure hope Abigail's is okay. He's a cool little dog."

"I'm sure he's fine," I said, deciding not to divulge what I knew for the moment. "Why the need for the big act?"

"Oh, you mean the plight of the working class and all that?" he said, managing a small smile.

"Yeah."

"Well, it does help a bit with the guilt," he said. "And you have to admit that the combination of a left-wing free paper that funds itself by selling ads to the very same businesses it constantly condemns has a nice ironic twist to it."

"I have to give you that," I said, laughing. "It does."

"But mostly I do it to just to annoy my old man. I keep spending his money while publishing a paper that regularly refers to people like him as disciples of the devil."

"Aren't you worried he's going to cut you off?"

"Nah, he can't touch me. My mom set up an irrevocable trust for me before she died. And as soon as I turned twenty-one, it was off to the races for me when it came to burning through it."

"But you haven't been able to spend it all?" I said, raising an eyebrow.

"Well, I'm sure I could if I tried hard enough," he said, frowning. "But between you and me, I like having it. Does that make me a despicable person?"

"I'd probably go with confused and leave it at that," I said. "It might help you sleep easier at night."

"No problem with that," he said, holding up his cookie. "After a couple of these, I sleep like a baby."

"Again, whatever works," I said, my neurons overloaded with new information. "I need to get going. But thanks for your time."

"No problem," he said, standing up and extending his hand. "And if you happen to run into Abigail, remind her that she still owes me some more articles. But since she's doing them for free, I don't have much leverage with her."

"She's not charging you for them?"

"No, she said that all that mattered was getting them out in print," he said.

"Interesting," I said, then another question popped into my head. "How did your father make his money?"

"He's a doctor. But several years ago, he got into real estate development. That's where he made most of his money."

"A doctor?" I said as another neuron fired hard. "Your last name isn't Couch by any chance, is it?"

"Yeah, it sure is. You know my dad?"

"I've met him a few times. He's a friend of my mother."

"Everybody knows each other down here. Especially those in the ruling class with means," he said, shrugging and allowing himself a momentary lapse back into revolutionary rhetoric. "He hates my guts. But I can't really blame him. I do everything I can to give him lots of reasons."

His last cookie seemed to kick in, and he began to drift away. I waved goodbye and left the office to the sound of an intergalactic battle playing out on his computer. I walked outside to my jeep, waving goodbye to Jessie on my way past her desk, and headed for the bakery to pick up a couple dozen chocolate chip cookies on my way home.

Even though they weren't the type of cookie that produced the ongoing urge to keep eating, I was pretty sure I could force down a half-dozen before I filled up.

My munchies didn't need any help.

Chapter 19

Captain Jack greeted us on the pier like we were long, lost friends, but I assumed the source of his excitement was driven more by the fact that he'd been spending the day on the water with the three of us instead of trying to avoid flying treble hooks while attempting to teach a boatload of tourists the finer points of deep sea fishing. We'd been talking about visiting Little Cayman and Cayman Brac, the other two islands that, along with Grand Cayman, comprised the Cayman Islands. We really couldn't consider ourselves residents, even part-timers, if we hadn't at least visited the other islands, so we agreed to set aside the day to explore and relax. After leaving all the dogs with my mother, we headed for Captain Jack's boat and a day out on the water.

Josie and Chef Claire were in the two-piece suits my mother had gotten them for Christmas, something that got Captain Jack's attention faster than a poorly thrown treble hook when they removed their shorts and tee shirts and stretched out in the sun. I had opted for full-coverage white linen and a floppy hat my mother said reminded her of Katherine Hepburn's outfit in *The African Queen*. The three of them could laugh all they wanted, and they did, but I wasn't taking any chances.

Little Cayman is located about eighty miles northeast of Grand Cayman, and Captain Jack told us to kick back and enjoy the ride that would take just under two hours. The early morning sun was already hot, the sky cloudless, but the breeze created by the boat's speed of forty knots, along with the cooler Chef Claire had packed, helped us relax. Josie removed one of the containers filled with a variety of sliced fruits and passed it around. Then she grabbed another, this one loaded with a bacon spinach quiche Chef Claire had brought home from the restaurant. I filled a small plate and stretched out and nibbled on a piece of mango.

"Are you sure you're okay with the two for one special?" I said to Chef Claire. "I sort of sprung that one on you."

"A little late to start worrying about that now, isn't it?" Josie said through a mouthful of quiche.

"No, it's fine," Chef Claire said. "Tuesday is a good night to do something like that. And it can't hurt to start bringing in some more first-timers."

"The place is off to a great start," Josie said. "And I really like Chef Finn."

"Yeah, he's great," Chef Claire said. "We'll be fine unless the police decide to arrest Rocco."

I thought about what she said. Even though Rocco was at work, the possibility of him being charged with the murder of Teresa's ex-husband definitely cast a shadow over what should be a very happy time for all of us.

"So, this guy Frederick is Dr. Couch's son?" Josie said, reaching for another slice of quiche.

"Yeah. I was surprised," I said, wiping mango juice off my mouth. "But I can see why his father might not want to talk about him. He's an odd duck. And a total stoner."

"You think he's somehow involved in this thing?" Josie said.

"No, I doubt it," I said, shaking my head. "He seems to spend his days getting high. And the thought of killing somebody would probably seem like too much work."

"Not to mention ruining his buzz," Josie said, grinning.

"Exactly," I said, reaching for a slice of quiche before it disappeared. "But we do know that this Abigail who wrote the article is the woman Captain rescued. And she is apparently also a woman of considerable means. Frederick said she just happened to show up and offer her services."

"A well-to-do environmentalist who travels the globe writing opinion pieces free of charge to anyone who'll print them?" Josie said, frowning. "Nah, that sounds way too convenient to be the whole story."

"I agree," I said, sliding back into partial shade. "There has to be a local connection somewhere. Maybe a development company or a family member she's got it in for."

"It's going to be a little hard to track it down given the fact you don't know her last name," Chef Claire said.

"Yeah, I know. I can't believe she got in and out of the hospital without using her real name or showing ID," I said. "But she also used an alias at the guesthouse where she was staying, so maybe it's not that hard to believe after all. I don't know. I'm at a loss."

"You'll figure it out, Snoopmeister," Josie said, gently punching me on the shoulder. "You always do. Did you ask this guy Frederick if the name Owen rang a bell?"

"No, I didn't," I said, chuckling. "I didn't want to confuse him. He was having a hard enough time remembering I was even in the office."

"I dated a stoner once," Josie said.

"How did that go?" Chef Claire said.

"I just told you. I dated him *once*."

"Got it," Chef Claire said, laughing.

"It wasn't so much that he was high," Josie said. "It was the smell. It was a chilly night, and he was wearing this thick wool sweater. Then it started raining, and we got soaked on our way to the restaurant. Did you know that hemp-scented, wet wool smells an awful lot like wet dog? It almost put me off my dinner."

"The operative word being *almost*," I said to Chef Claire.

"Funny. So, what's the plan going forward?" Josie said, reaching into a cooler for bottles of water she passed out.

"When in doubt, poke the bear," I said, shrugging.

"Oh, good one. That's always highly entertaining to watch. Which bear do you plan on poking?" Josie said.

"I thought I'd start with Dr. Couch," I said. "I doubt if there's anything there, but I'm thinking that if I can get him talking about his son, something might shake loose that could be useful."

"You know that this Abigail might be residing on the bottom of the ocean by now, don't you?" Josie said softly.

"Yes, I do. But it's too early to quit looking for her," I said. "She must be involved in all this land activity in some way. And we really can't give her dog away to my mom until we have a better idea what happened to her."

"Good luck getting that dog away from your mother," Josie said. "Earl's like a ten-pound lump of fur that's growing out of her lap."

"That's the King Charles for you. They were basically bred to be lapdogs," I said.

"Well, then that little guy was certainly very well-bred," Chef Claire said, shaking her head. "They're inseparable."

I nodded in agreement. My mother, once someone who only tolerated dogs and my lifelong commitment to them, was now a card-carrying devotee of the fabulous four-legged creatures that dominated our lives.

"Who else are you going to poke if you don't get anything out of Dr. Couch?" Josie said, apparently torn about whether to have a third piece of quiche or not. She broke the corner off one of the pieces and tossed it into her mouth.

"You do know it still counts even if you only eat it a bite at a time while it's still in the container, right?" Chef Claire said, giving her a coy smile.

"Oh, you caught that?" she said, breaking off another corner before refocusing on me. "Are you going to pay Gerald another visit?"

"I'm never going back to that office," I said, shaking my head.

"Why not?" she deadpanned. "The hard part is already over." She paused to grin at Chef Claire. "You know, the part about getting naked in front of him."

I sat quietly fuming and did my best to ignore her.

"Just wear that outfit, and you'll be fine," Josie said, laughing. "What did your mother call it?"

"Victorian-beekeeper," Chef Claire said, shaking her head. "Sometimes your mom really cracks me up."

"Yeah, she's a real hoot," I said. "If and when I need to speak with Gerald again it will be in a public place."

"I'm sure the two of you will be able to find a nice secluded stretch of sand somewhere," Josie deadpanned.

I glared at her, then called out to Captain Jack.

"Are we there yet?"

Chapter 20

Captain Jack slowed the boat as the island known as Little Cayman came into view, and he effortlessly transitioned from boat captain into tour guide. Reciting from memory, he told us that the island was about ten miles long and up to a mile wide in some spots. I kept waiting for the island to rise up from the sea as we got closer, but the landmass continued to hover just above the water.

"If rising sea levels are a reality," Josie said as if reading my mind, "this place is in a whole lot of trouble."

"Without a doubt," I said, glancing over the side of the boat to watch a sea turtle that was gliding through the shallow water. "How many people live here?"

"I think it's around two hundred," Captain Jack said.

"Talk about your remote lifestyle," I said, shaking my head at the prospect of living on such a small patch of sand and rock in the middle of the ocean.

"You want remote?" Captain Jack said, pointing at what appeared to be a small island just off the southwest corner of Little Cayman. "Now, that's what I call remote."

He turned the boat toward the small islet to offer us a better view. We looked at the pristine patch of sand and natural vegetation.

"There's nothing on it?" Josie said, holding her hand up to block the glare.

"No," Captain Jack said, coming to a complete stop and drifting. "It's completely undeveloped. And the only way to get there is by boat. Most people kayak over. I guess you could swim it, but I wouldn't recommend it. People rent kayaks on Little Cayman and spend the day over there having a picnic or doing whatever strikes their fancy. If you get my drift."

"Got it," I said, nodding as I continued to stare at it.

"It's also a place where some people get married."

"That sounds pretty romantic," I said, continuing to scan the island.

"That's what they say," Captain Jack said, nodding. "And I see the occasional yacht anchored offshore and people heading for the island in dinghies."

"It's gorgeous. How long does it take to paddle across from Little Cayman?"

"Only about fifteen minutes or so," he said. "It's not bad at all. Unless the wind is up. But you have to bring everything with you. I think of this place every time I watch that movie Castaway."

"There you go, Gilligan," Josie said. "The perfect getaway spot for you and Gerald to get better acquainted."

"Will you please stop?"

"Yeah, it's a pretty special place," Captain Jack said, nodding. "A trip to Owen Island is right at the top of a lot of people's list of things to do when they visit.

I flinched like Chef Claire had hit me right between the eyes with her softball bat. I glanced back and forth at both of them. They hadn't missed the reference either.

"Did you say *Owen* Island?" I said, staring at Captain Jack.

"Yeah. What about it?" he said, frowning.

"Does the government own it?" I said.

"No, I think it's privately owned," he said. "But whoever does own it must be pretty cool. There are signs on the island that say *Welcome* instead of *Private Property* or *No Trespassing*. It's just one of those magical untouched spots that help you believe there might be some hope for the environment."

"And the owner has never tried to develop it?" I said, my neurons colliding all over the place.

"I don't think so," he said, shaking his head. "But I imagine all hell would break loose if anybody ever tried."

"Is it possible this is what she was talking about?" I said, glancing back and forth at Josie and Chef Claire.

"People trying to buy up blocks of vacant land and being very secretive about it. And an environmentalist writing negative articles about it who mysteriously disappears," Josie said. "Yeah, I can make the connection."

"But why all the subterfuge? If they want to buy and develop this place, why not just do it and be done with it?" Chef Claire said.

"They'd probably need the government's permission to do it," I said.

"And didn't Gerald say that they're getting enough heat already from the residents and environmental groups about unchecked development?" Josie said.

"He did," I said, squinting hard to force the ideas and questions bouncing around my head into coherent thoughts.

"Then building on this place might be enough to turn the current criticism into public outrage," Josie said.

"It would have to," I said, concentrating hard. Then a lightbulb popped that was bright enough to light a night sky when I flashed back to something else Gerald had mentioned in passing. "Unless it was only one component of a very complicated deal."

"I just lost the plot," Josie said, shrugging.

"Yeah, me too," Chef Claire said.

I continued to stare at the small island as my mind continued to race.

"Uh-oh," Chef Claire said. "She's got that look."

"Yeah, she's a goner," Josie said, then turned to Captain Jack. "She's gonna be a while. What sort of restaurants do they have on Little Cayman?"

"I always go to the Hungry Iguana," Captain Jack said. "Conch fritters and Mudslides. What's not to like?"

"Then what are we doing sitting out here in the middle of the ocean?" Josie said, laughing.

"Is she okay?" Captain Jack said, glancing over at me.

"She'll be fine," Chef Claire said. "The batteries in her neurons generally run down after about ten minutes."

"What?"

"Nothing," Chef Claire said, shaking her head, then glancing at me. "Suzy?"

"Yeah?"

"We're going to head to shore and eat lunch," she said.

"Okay. I could eat."

"See?" Chef Claire said, grinning at Captain Jack. "She's fine."

"I guess I'm gonna have to take your word for it."

Chapter 21

There's a very important day that falls about a week after Christmas, and we never miss the chance to celebrate it with friends and family. I know you probably think I'm referring to New Year's Eve, but that's tomorrow. December 30th is National Bacon Day. And while we're not going as overboard on the menu as we would have back home in Clay Bay, we're still marking the day with a bacon-fest barbecue at our place.

The party was an excellent excuse to invite Dr. Couch and hopefully get him in a relaxed mood where he'd be comfortable talking about his son. He hadn't arrived yet, but he'd promised my mother he'd drop by as soon as he completed his evening rounds at the hospital. She was sitting at a table on the lawn chatting with Gerald, John Smith, and a few other people I'd seen before but did not know. Rocco and Teresa had taken her girls and Captain and Chloe for a stroll on the beach. They'd invited Chef Claire's Goldens to join them, but as soon as Al and Dente got a whiff of the smells coming off the grill, they plopped themselves down at Chef Claire's feet and made it clear they weren't going anywhere.

I was stretched out in one of the recliners sipping a Mudslide and trying to decide whether to start with my traditional bacon cheeseburger or stretch my wings a bit and go with a couple of the chicken and bacon quesadillas drizzled with a bacon-bourbon cream sauce that was a total knee-buckler. But before I could decide, Chef Claire walked by with a tray of bacon-wrapped jalapeno poppers that caught my attention.

"Get them while they're hot," she said, extending the tray.

"Thanks. Do you need any help?" I said, selecting two of the poppers.

"No, we're all set," she said, glancing around. "I'm just going to pass these out then I'll join you. Henry has got the grill covered."

"How's your sunburn?" I said, grinning at her.

"It hurts," she said, gently rubbing her free hand over the back of her thighs. "I guess that's what we get for laughing at you. Save me a seat."

I watched her stroll off with the tray and munched on one of the poppers. I spotted Josie coming out onto the patio and doing her best to look casual. But I knew she was hurting. She waved to my mother as she stepped outside, closed the screen door behind her, then eased her way onto the recliner next to me.

"How you doing?" I said, casually.

"Oh, I'm fine," she said, wincing.

"Yes, I can see that," I deadpanned. "I have some more of that Aloe Vera lotion if you want it. I'm sure Captain Jack would be more than happy to rub it in."

"Okay, go ahead. Knock yourself out," she said, gingerly moving around to get comfortable. "I deserve it."

"I told you to cover up," I said, shaking my head. "I distinctively remember saying, Josie, you're going to get burned. Don't you remember me telling you that? Because I certainly remember saying it. At least three different times. But what do I know, right?"

"Suzy?"

"Yeah."

"You're being very annoying."

"Good. That's what I was going for."

I noticed Dr. Couch coming through the gate off the front of the house. He glanced around, caught my mother's eye and waved, then headed for the makeshift bar we'd set up.

"Save a recliner for Chef Claire," I said, getting to my feet. "I'm going to go have a little chat with Dr. Couch."

I walked across the lawn toward the bar. Dr. Couch saw me coming and greeted me with a warm smile.

"Thanks so much for the invitation," he said, opening a beer. "National Bacon Day? As a cardiologist, I suppose I should thank you for your marketing efforts on my behalf." He laughed loudly at his own joke and took a long pull from his beer. "Any excuse for a party, huh?"

"Bacon Day is sacred around our house," I said, laughing. "Say, can I have a word with you?"

"Of course," he said.

I headed for an empty table near the shallow end of the pool, and we sat down. He took a sip, set the bottle down, then folded his hands and looked at me.

"What's up?"

"I recently met your son," I said, going for casual. "We had quite a chat."

"Really? I do hope it didn't ruin your day," he said, surprised by the news. "How did you manage to run into him?"

"Well, I've been doing some...*research* in the hope of tracking down the woman who owns the King Charles spaniel that's staying with my mom."

"Research?" he said, grinning at me with raised eyebrows.

"It's a nicer word than snooping," I said, shrugging.

"Yes, it is," he said, laughing. "Please, continue."

"Anyway, I came across an article that was focused on the battle between the environmentalists and developers as well as various land deals and some of the companies who might be involved."

"I see," he said without emotion. "You're referring to the article in that disgusting rag my son likes to call a newspaper."

"I take it you're not a big fan of *The People's Paradise*."

He snorted contempt and shook his head as he stared off at the surf.

"Was he smoking weed when you met with him?"

"No," I said. "But he was eating cookies."

"I see. Well, I suppose his lungs appreciated the break," he said, flatly. "What did he have to say?"

"Not much, really. He made a few token references to the worker's struggles, laid out a bit of his personal history, then got back to his cookies and video game."

"Lenin would be so proud," Dr. Couch said, not even bothering to hide his disdain.

"Yeah, I have to say that his commitment to the cause appears to be a bit situational," I said. "Not to mention being driven by self-interest and a genuine desire to poke you in the eye with a sharp stick."

"That sums it up quite well," he said, nodding. "But there's nothing I can do about it. His mother made sure of that before she passed."

"Yes, he did mention the irrevocable trust," I said.

"I see," he said, nodding. "Did he mention anything else?"

"Well, he did confirm the identity of the woman we rescued on the beach. It turns out she was the one who wrote the article."

"Interesting," he said, nodding.

"And she's still missing," I said. "Or at least I can't find her. We still have her dog. Are you sure she didn't give you any other information while she was in the hospital? Even her last name might help me track her down."

"No, she didn't," he said, shaking his head. "After we spoke about it on Christmas Day, I had the staff take another look. We probably should have pressed her for more details about her identity, but she was totally coherent when we discharged her, and she paid her bill in cash. The staff didn't think it was that important. And since it was Christmas and she made it very clear she needed to get somewhere, they did everything they could to accommodate her."

"Okay," I said, exhaling loudly. "I guess I'll just have to keep looking."

"I wish I could help you, Suzy," he said, again staring out at the ocean. "So, my son was completely stoned?"

"Yeah, pretty much. But I have to say that it didn't seem to affect his gaming skills," I said, laughing.

"What a waste of a life," he said, managing a sad shake of his head.

"Has he always had an interest in, what do I call it, the plight of the workers?" I said, placing my elbows on the table and leaning forward.

"No, of course not," he said, frowning. "That particular scam came to him later in life."

"Scam?"

"He figured out that having money and posing as a radical was a great way to pick up women," he said. "Frederick memorized and began reciting famous revolutionary quotes to impressionable young girls who were down here on vacation. And the fact that he was able to afford a lot of good drugs made his job that much easier. Then he got the idea to start publishing that rag sheet to give himself some additional *street-cred*. The fact that it drives me crazy and is a constant source of embarrassment to many of my friends was just icing on the cake for him."

"Frederick mentioned that you made your fortune in real estate," I said.

"He was in a chatty mood, wasn't he?" Dr. Couch said, grinning at me. "Yes, I've been very fortunate. Years ago, I was looking for some investment opportunities, and I happened to meet Gerald and your mother along with a few other investors."

"I take it this was before Gerald got into politics?"

"Oh, way before. Back then, Gerald was just another entrepreneur looking to hit it big," he said. "And he did. Fortunately, he brought a lot of us along with him for the ride."

"I see," I said, trying to juggle several thoughts. "Are you still active in that world?"

"Actually, I've been looking for a way to cut back," he said, shrugging. "I'm dealing with some health issues at the moment, and my doctor wants me to eliminate as much stress as possible."

"*Your* doctor," I said, smiling. "That's funny. It's sort of like lawyers trying to represent themselves, right?"

"Exactly," he said, nodding. "And there's a word for doctors who try to perform self-diagnosis."

"Dead?"

"Your mother was right," he said with a booming laugh. "Nothing gets past you."

"What sort of health problems are you dealing with?"

"I have a bad heart," he said, shrugging.

"I'm sorry to hear that. Does Frederick know?"

"No, and there's no point telling him. I'm afraid he doesn't believe I even have one."

"I can't imagine what that must be like," I said, shaking my head. "I don't know what I'd do without my mother."

"I've gotten used to the idea," he said, again staring out at the ocean.

"Do you have any other family members around?"

"No, just Frederick. My plan has always been to leave everything to him when I'm gone."

"And that's changed?"

He grabbed his beer off the table and stood.

"Let's say that it remains to be seen how much I'll be leaving him and leave it at that." He glanced over at the table where my mother was holding court. "I should head over there and say hello."

"I'm so sorry to hear the news about your health, Dr. Couch," I said, getting up from my chair. "I hope it all eventually works out."

"Thank you, Suzy. You're very kind," he said, waving as he headed off.

For some reason, my neurons continued to fire as I watched him sit back down and join the conversation at the table. Given everything he'd just told me, I couldn't imagine what remained to be seen when it came to his son's inheritance.

Maybe he was still holding out hope that he and his son might be able to reconcile before his bad ticker finally gave out.

Maybe he was considering the possibility of leaving everything to charity.

Then a lightbulb popped, and I visibly flinched.

Or maybe he didn't have nearly as much money as everyone assumed he did.

Chapter 22

"I understand you'd like to see the list of registered marriages."

"Yes."

"How far back are we talking about? Six months? Maybe a year?"

"Well, I was originally thinking 1975, but just to be sure maybe we should go back to 1970."

The clerk who worked at the General Registry, the official public records office of the Cayman Islands, blinked and gave me an open-mouth stare. I couldn't blame her. Even for me, the thought that I might be able to make some progress by identifying marriages that had taken place on Owen Island bordered on insanity. Eventually, she found her voice.

"You want to see every registered marriage since 1970?"

"Yes." I smiled and nodded then remembered my mother's admonition, instilled in me from a very young age, to always use the magic word. "Please."

"You do realize that many of those records pre-date the installment of our computer records system," the clerk said, cocking her head at me.

"I did not know that," I said, shrugging. "But surely they're all written down somewhere. You must have copies of the marriage certificates, right?"

"We do," the clerk, still managing to maintain her cool. "But the really old records are only entered into the computer on an individual basis."

"You lost me," I said with a frown.

"When we put the computer records system in, we decided to only bring over summary totals of some items. Permits, business licenses, things like that. Old marriage certificates were one of those items. I can tell you how many people got married each year, and I might be able to tell you how many couples each registered Marriage Officer married. But if we need the information about a specific marriage from those days we usually have to go into our paper archives to look for it."

"Why would you need information about a specific marriage?"

"Sometimes it's needed for a divorce proceeding or a death notice. Occasionally we'll get a request from overseas when a copy is needed to verify the marriage," the clerk said. "It could be for any number of reasons."

"I see. And why didn't you just enter them all into the new system when you put it in?" I said.

"Because we were incredibly busy, often frantic, just trying to get the new system in, and back then, it seemed like a major waste of time," she said, giving me a tight-lipped smile. "But if I had known all those years ago that you'd be coming in today, I might have decided differently."

"There's no need to get snarky," I said, frowning.

"You don't know the year of the marriage you're looking for?"

"No."

"Do you know the name of the Marriage Officer who performed the ceremony?"

"Not a clue," I said, shaking my head. "What's a Marriage Officer?"

"They're individuals who are registered with the government and approved to perform marriages. Usually, they're clergy members of local churches, but we do have a handful who aren't attached to any specific denomination."

"I see," I said with a frown. "It's a bit more complicated than I imagined."

"Yes, and the one you're looking for is probably on paper and stored in a cardboard box," she said with a coy smile. "If the marriage took place after we installed the computer system."

"When was that?"

"I'd have to check to get the actual date, but it was sometime in the early 90's."

"My guess is that the wedding I'm looking for took place before that. But I really can't be sure," I said.

"This wedding?" she said. "Family, friend, friend of the family?"

"No," I said, shaking my head. "Nothing like that. It's pretty much a wild-goose chase at the moment. You know, grasping at straws."

"I see."

"How long will it take you to go through your archives?"

"Well, if I got started straight away and dropped everything else I'm supposed to be doing, I could probably get it done in about a week."

"But you're not going to drop everything else, are you?" I said, forcing a small smile.

"No, I'm not," she said, shaking her head. "And if the Finance Minister hadn't called me personally requesting that I speak with you, our conversation would have ended soon after it began."

"Sure, sure."

"Can I ask you why the Finance Minister made that call?"

"Well, Gerald sort of owes me a favor," I said, deciding to go with a small white lie.

"I see," she said, studying my face closely. Then her eyes grew wide, and she couldn't keep the grin off her face. "You're the woman who got caught in his office with her pants down, aren't you?"

My face flushed deep red, and it brought back all sorts of sunburn memories, especially the humiliating experience I'd had in Gerald's office. I took a deep breath, managed to make eye contact with her, and gave her a small nod.

"I'm not sure *caught* is the correct term," I whispered.

"Well, from what I've heard," she said with a giggle. "He certainly does owe you a favor."

"Funny," I said, glaring at her. "Okay, you've made your point."

"How did you manage to find the nerve to do that in his office?" she said with genuine interest. "I could never do that. I'd be scared to death of getting caught. Are you one of those people who enjoys doing things like that in public places?"

"I think we're done here," I said, getting up from my chair.

"We'll get started reviewing the archives as soon as we can," she said, still grinning. "Should I call you when it's ready or just leave a message with *Ger-ald*?"

"You're enjoying this way too much," I said, beaten. "Where did you hear about it?"

"It's a small island," she said, shrugging. "Wait until I tell everyone I've met Gerald's mystery woman."

"Oh, I really wish you wouldn't," I said, heading toward the door. Then I stopped when another thought popped into my head. "Is the location of the wedding listed on your marriage certificates?"

"These days, most certainly," she said. "But back then, the location could have either specifically mentioned the island it took place on, or it might have only referenced the Cayman Islands. Things were a little looser back then, and I imagine each

Marriage Officer had their own system for how they recorded things like that."

"So, there could have been weddings on Little Cayman that weren't identified as having taken place on the island?"

"I'm sure there were," she said, nodding. "The wedding you're looking for took place on Little Cayman?"

"Yes. At least that's my thinking at the moment," I said.

"Then you might want to speak with the Marriage Officer on the island," she said, leaning back in her chair.

"There's one on Little Cayman?"

"I'm pretty sure the pastor of the church on Little Cayman is a registered Marriage Officer. There's only one on the island."

"You know, that's a pretty good idea," I said, nodding at her.

"Better than digging through thirty years of paper archives?"

"Well, let's call that our backup plan. Sort of an insurance policy to make sure we find it," I said, giving her a snarky grin. "We'd hate to disappoint the Finance Minister, right?"

"Yes, we certainly would," she said, glaring at me. "But I imagine you'd know more about how to disappoint him than I would."

"Funny. And for the record, that whole thing in the office was an accident," I said, brushing my hair back from my face.

"My shorts fell down, and when I bent down to pull them up, I tripped over them and fell."

"I see," she said, not believing a word coming out of my mouth. "If I'm ever caught in a compromising situation, I'll have to try to remember that one. It's much better than I just slipped on a banana peel."

"I'm going to leave now," I said, making a face at her. "The archives await. Happy hunting."

"You, too."

I left the office before I gave in to the urge to knock the goofy grin she was giving me off her face. On my way toward the front door, I crossed paths with a woman who was entering the building and talking on her phone. When I drew near, she stared at me and gave me the once-over.

"She's right here," the woman whispered into her phone. "Yeah, white blouse, tan shorts. It's her." She shot me a quick glance as I walked past her. "Yeah, she is attractive. He's doing well for being such an old dog, isn't he?"

Her laughter followed me out the door. Apparently, the story of my encounter with Gerald in his office was about to spread further across the island like an out of control wildfire. I suppose I could have obsessed about being identified and subsequently judged as one of the Finance Minister's girlfriends, dalliances, or worse.

But my neurons were preoccupied with another obsession at the moment. I believed I was getting close to uncovering at least part of the mystery I'd had no luck solving. And I knew I still needed some help. As well as a bit of luck.

I also needed one more thing.

I needed a ride.

Chapter 23

"You're on Captain Jack's boat?" Josie said into the phone.

"Yeah, I'm heading back to Little Cayman," I said, having to speak loudly over the noise of the engine.

"Should I even ask why?" she said, also trying to make herself heard over the background noise she was dealing with.

"No, I'll tell you all about it later. Where the heck are you?"

"I'm at the shelter helping Teresa get ready for the opening. We just got a bunch of dogs and cats delivered, and Dr. Seltzer's flight was delayed again. Apparently, there's bad weather in Florida, and the airlines are really backed up. So Teresa asked me to come over and do some exams and shots. You wouldn't believe the adorable litter of puppies that was just brought in. They can't be more than eight weeks old."

"Wish I could be there," I shouted. "I said, I wish I could be there…Never mind. I'll talk with you later."

I ended the call and slipped my phone back into my shorts. I sat down on the seat next to Captain Jack.

"What's Josie up to?"

"She's spending the day surrounded by animals," I said, glancing over at him.

"So, she's in heaven, right?" he said, laughing.

"Pretty much," I said, adjusting my sunglasses as I settled into my seat and stared out at the magnificent stretch of ocean surrounding me. "But being out here comes pretty close, too. Thanks for fitting me in on short notice."

"It's not a problem. This was supposed to be my day off, but since I usually spend it out on the water, I might as well get paid to do it."

Unable to argue with his logic, I stretched out and pulled my hat down low to protect my face from the sun. The constant drone of the engine coupled with the breeze soon lulled me to sleep, and when I woke up, I could see Little Cayman on the horizon.

"You were out," Captain Jack said.

"I know," I said, yawning. "You sure this church is easy to find?"

"You're joking, right?" he said, laughing. "Yeah, I'm pretty sure you'll find it. I'll wait for you at the Hungry Iguana."

"Okay. Are you sure I'll be able to walk it?" I said, glancing out at the rapidly approaching shoreline.

"Well, I certainly hope so," he said chuckling as he pulled the throttle back until the boat was in neutral. "If you don't mind, can you handle the bow line?"

"That I can do," I said, getting up from my seat and arching my back.

When we had docked, I hopped out, tied off the bow and stern, then stared out at Owen Island while I waited for Captain

Jack. We walked down the dock then waved as we headed off in different directions. I walked toward a section of town called Blossom Village, which was apparently the spot where the original inhabitants had taken up residence. A small number of buildings dotted the area along with several wooden houses I assumed were historical. A handful of tourist resorts were located nearby as were what appeared to be a couple of condo complexes. All in all, it was a pretty idyllic setting, and I soon came upon a small church.

A large lizard was sitting on the front steps staring up at me. On my way to the church, I'd passed a road sign that told me in no uncertain terms that iguanas had the right of way. Even though I wasn't driving, I veered to my right and kept my distance from the Blue Iguana that must have been four feet long.

I entered, gave my eyes time to adjust to the change in light, then glanced around the empty space. I slowly walked toward the front of the church and heard a noise off to my right. I cleared my throat, and a man turned around, saw me standing there and beamed at me.

"Welcome," he said, heading toward me.

"Am I in the right place?" I said.

"Are you seeking the comfort and solace of a house of worship?" he said, his smile etched on.

"Well, no, not per se," I said, frowning. "But I am looking for a church. And the comfort and solace part would be a nice bonus." I gave him a weak smile.

"Then you are definitely in the right place. We're the only game in town," he said, laughing.

"What's the deal with the lizard out front?" I said, nodding toward the front door.

"Oh, that's George," the man said. "We've sort of adopted him."

"They're protected, right?"

"Yes, and making quite a comeback. There are more iguanas on the island than people."

"They're cute. In a little lizardy sort of way. My name is Suzy Chandler," I said, extending my hand.

"It's nice to meet you, Suzy," he said, giving me an energetic handshake. "I'm Pastor Roy. How can I help you?"

"I'm trying to get some information about a wedding," I said, glancing around.

"Well, congratulations. I'm sure that you'll be very happy and find great satisfaction in the sanctity of marriage. And I hope that you and your husband will soon grace both your families with some wonderful grandchildren."

"You been talking to my mother, Pastor?" I said, cocking my head at him.

"What?"

"Nothing," I said, shaking my head. "Forget it. I think it's just a reflex response I've developed. Like a nervous tic. You see, Pastor, my mother is really starting to put the pressure on. And I want to give her at least one grandkid, but I haven't met anybody I'd consider settling down with. Well, I've met a few, but something always seems to come up or get in the way. I'm sure you know what I mean. You must get that sort of thing all the time."

I paused to take a breath. Apparently, I must have paid some attention during church when I was a young Catholic girl. I guess some lessons really stick: Walk into church, search one's soul, and start confessing. I forced another smile at him.

"No, the wedding isn't mine," I said. "This is about a wedding that might have taken place a while ago."

"I see," he said, giving me a confused look, apparently now unsure how good a candidate for motherhood I actually was. "When was the wedding?"

"You see, that's the problem. I'm not sure."

"Okay, and you came here seeking enlightenment?" he deadpanned.

I stared at him, then got the joke.

"Oh, good one," I said, laughing. "Well, if that's what I was going for, this would be the place, right?"

"It's certainly a good place to start," he said, gesturing for me to take a seat. "Why don't you tell me a bit about your dilemma?"

"I'm trying to track down someone who I think might have gotten married on Owen Island," I said.

"It's fairly common for people to exchange vows on the island," he said, nodding. "And it seems to be gaining in popularity. I've performed several ceremonies there myself."

"I think this one might have happened twenty or even thirty years ago," I said. "Maybe even longer."

"Then I doubt if I'll be able to help you," he said, shrugging. "I'm relatively new. But you might want to check with the General Registry over on Grand Cayman. They're responsible for keeping track of all the public records."

"Yeah, I've already been there," I said, frowning. "And they said they're going to go through their archives when they get a chance."

"I would have thought they'd have it in their computer system," he said, surprised.

"That's what I thought," I said, placing a hand on his forearm. "But apparently a lot of the older records are still on paper."

"And it's going to take them some time to pull all the records."

"Yes."

"But you're in a rush to find it now and just can't wait, right?"

"You have been talking to my mother, haven't you?" I said, laughing.

"Let's call it a lucky guess," he said. "I'm sorry, but I've never seen a master list of all the weddings that have taken place here on the island. I write them down in my marriage book and send all the information to the General Registry."

"Well, it was worth a shot," I said, getting up. "Thanks for your time."

"You know, I have an idea. It's a bit of a long shot, but since you're here, it might be worth checking out."

"What do you suggest?" I said.

"You might want to pay Pastor Tim a visit. He lives in one of the old historical homes you probably saw on your way here."

"Pastor Tim?"

"Yes, he's a wonderful man. He was the pastor here for decades. But I doubt if he'll be able to remember anything useful." Pastor Roy flashed a sad smile. "He's getting up there years. He just turned ninety, and I'm afraid his mind isn't what it used to be. It's quite sad to watch. But he's had a remarkable life."

"Dementia? Alzheimer's?" I said, frowning and immediately feeling empathy for the stranger.

"I'm not sure of the official diagnosis at this point. But he is certainly dealing with some very difficult symptoms. About a year ago, we decided to help him out with a live-in housekeeper."

"Are you sure it would be okay if I stopped by?"

"I think he would love it," he said, walking with me as I headed toward the door. "It will give him a chance to reminisce and tell some of his stories again." Pastor Roy chuckled. It was soft and sad. "I'm afraid I've heard all of his stories more times than I can remember."

"I'm sorry to hear that. I hate seeing that happen," I said.

"Yes, well, I'm afraid that it's one of the challenges that often come with living a very long life," he said. "He's a wonderful man. I just hope you catch him on a good day."

I shook hands with him and followed the directions he gave me. The directions weren't really necessary, and a few minutes later I walked down a short stone path toward a wooden house that sat a short walk from the beach. The house was small and weathered, but well-preserved and inviting. I tapped on the screen door, and a middle-aged, dark-skinned woman came to the door.

"Hello," she said, pleasantly. "Can I help you?"

"Hi, my name is Suzy Chandler. I was wondering if it would be possible for me to speak with Pastor Tim?"

"Are you a friend of his?" she said, casually giving me the once over from the other side of the screen.

"Actually, no. But Pastor Roy suggested I stop by. I'm trying to gather some information about a wedding that took place years ago."

"I see," she said, giving my request some thought. "Well, he is having a good day. Just give me a moment. Let me go check to see if he feels up to it."

"Thanks," I said, then turned around to take another look at Owen Island. I rocked back and forth on my heels and wondered what it would be like to exchange marriage vows on a deserted island. At a minimum, the island setting would provide the perfect insurance policy for a couple just in case one of them got cold feet at the last minute. As far as I was concerned, if faced with the choice of going through with the wedding or swimming back to shore with the sharks, I was pretty sure I'd take my chances on the marriage. I turned back around when I heard the woman approach.

"Pastor Tim said he would love to talk with you. Please, come in."

She opened the screen door, and I stepped inside. I noticed a small, bald man sitting in an overstuffed chair staring at me. He used both hands to push himself up out of the chair and extended his hand. I'd been expecting a dark-skinned man, but he was pale white and had sparkling blue eyes that bore into me. I returned the handshake and smiled at him.

"I can see you weren't expecting me to be one of the white-devils," he said with a soft cackle.

He was correct. I hadn't. The white part. Not the devil thing.

"It's so nice to meet you, Pastor Tim," I said, for some reason embarrassed by my assumption about his skin color. "I'm Suzy Chandler."

"It's very nice to meet you, Suzy," he said, gesturing for me to sit down. I sunk into one of the overstuffed chairs and he sat back down. "To answer one of your questions, I arrived years ago as a young pastor from the midwest on a mission to *tame the natives* and never left." He let loose with a booming laugh that belied his age. "Isn't that right, Shirley?"

"Listen to you," Shirley said, shaking her head at him with a look of affection. Then she glanced over at me. "Don't believe a word this old charlatan tells you." She slid a pillow behind him, waited until he smiled up at her to indicate he was comfortable, then nodded. "Okay, you two have fun. I'll be in the kitchen if you need me."

We both watched her depart then Pastor Tim glanced over at me.

"She takes such good care of me," he said. "But don't tell her that." He winked at me. "Truth be told, most days I need all the help I can get."

"I don't know if I'd say that, Pastor. You seem pretty spry to me," I said, grinning.

"I'm afraid spry is the least of my concerns," he said, suddenly turning serious. "I often feel like my mind is swimming in fog." He stared at me. "Does that make any sense to you?"

"Sure, I get that," I said, nodding. "But I can't imagine what it must be like if it never clears up ."

"I can't complain," he said, now turning philosophical. "I've been blessed with a very long life, and I've spent it in this beautiful place surrounded by a wonderful family and many, many friends."

"You can't ask for much more than that, right?" I said, enjoying the cross breeze that was spilling in through the open windows.

"One can always ask for more," he said, chuckling. "Like being able to remember what I had for breakfast. But enough about me and my problems. I can't imagine you came all this way to hear my thoughts about the meaning of life or the challenges of old age. How can I help you?"

"I'm trying to track down a wedding that might have taken place on Owen Island several years ago."

"I see," he said, squinting at me. "Can I ask you why?"

"This is going to sound pretty crazy," I said, frowning.

"Don't worry about that. In my line of work, I get that all the time," he said, cutting loose with a loud cackle.

"Okay," I said, smiling and leaning forward in my chair. "I think it might have something to do with a woman's disappearance. And a murder."

He frowned and placed both hands on the arms of his chair.

"Oh, my. Please, continue," he said softly.

I spent a few minutes giving him the short version of the events that had brought me here. He listened closely and seemed to be following the thread of the story. When I finished, I sat back in my chair and waited for him to respond.

"Shirley?" he called out eventually.

Shirley came out of the kitchen drying her hands on a dish towel.

"Yes?"

"Am I imagining it, or did Bess Campbell call recently?" Pastor Tim said, squinting at his housekeeper.

"As a matter of fact, she did," Shirley said. "I believe it was a few weeks ago. Well done, Pastor Tim."

"And you thought I'd completely lost it," he said, cackling. "I knew I remembered her calling."

"Who's Bess Campbell?" I said, glancing back and forth at them.

"She's the owner of Owen Island," Pastor Tim said. "At least she is at the moment. She's getting ready to sell it."

My neurons woke up and protested as they sluggishly got into gear. Must be too much sun, I decided.

"Did she happen to mention who she's selling it to?" I said.

"I believe she did," Pastor Tim said, frowning. "But I can't remember the name for the life of me. It was some company, I think. Do you remember, Shirley?"

"I remember you mentioning the name after you finished talking to her, but I can't recall it at the moment," she said, shaking her head. "But it definitely wasn't the name of a person."

"Why is she selling the island?" I said.

"Like me, Bess is getting up there in years," he said, shrugging. Then he stared off into the distance as if remembering a fond memory from the distant past. "And she simply isn't able to get down here anymore. It must be, what would you say, Shirley, at least ten years since we've seen her?"

"At least," Shirley said.

"She's trying to get her affairs in order," Pastor Tim said. "And she said the offer was just too much money to refuse."

"I need to get back to the kitchen," Shirley said. "I'm roasting a chicken, and I'd hate to overcook it. Would you like to stay for dinner?"

"No, thank you, Shirley. That's very kind, but I'll need to get back to Grand Cayman."

"Roast chicken, again?" Pastor Tim, said, scowling. "We just had it yesterday."

"That was a week ago," Shirley said softly with a shake of her head.

"It was?" he said, frowning. "Time flies, huh?" He cackled again and shrugged his bony shoulders at me.

If I was ever stricken with his malady at some point later in life, I hoped I'd be able to deal with it as well as he seemed to be handling it. Shirley strolled back into the kitchen, and I looked over at Pastor Tim who was deep in thought.

"I could have sworn we had chicken yesterday," he said. "Oh, well. Lucky for me, I love chicken."

"Me too," I said, nodding. "Did you perform some marriage ceremonies on Owen Island?"

"Of course," he said, smiling at me. "They used to only happen occasionally, but as the area became more popular with visitors, they increased in number."

I hated myself for having to ask the next question, but I couldn't come up with any way to avoid it.

"Do you remember conducting any ceremonies back in the Seventies and Eighties?"

"I do," he said, nodding. "But no specific ones come to mind. I remember they were always a lot of fun. Very special."

I frowned and drifted off as my thoughts began to steamroll and collide. I sat quietly and let them do their work for several moments then shrugged.

"Then I guess I'll just have to wait for the General Registry to finish their research," I said out loud to myself.

"There's no need to do that," he said, staring at me.

"I'm sorry. What did you say?" I said, refocusing on him.

"I said there's no need to wait for the folks at General Registry to find time for you. In my experience, like most bureaucracies, they tend to move at their own pace," he said. "I remember this one time when I had to wait forever for a…no, that wasn't General Registry. That was…who the heck was that?

196

Oh, well. It's probably not important." He stared at me, bemused. "What was I saying?"

"You were saying something about my not having to wait for General Registry to finish their work," I said, leaning forward in my chair.

"Of course," he said, nodding. "No need to do that. I'll just check my marriage book." He glanced toward the kitchen. "Shirley!"

"You kept your marriage book?" I said, my neurons suddenly firing on all cylinders.

"Yes, I did," he said, smiling. "My plan is to bequeath it to the museum. You probably saw it on your way over. It's right next to the church."

"I did notice it."

"What now?" Shirley said, doing her best to feign annoyance.

"Could you please grab my marriage book from the bookshelf?"

"If I burn the chicken, it's going to be your fault," she said, laughing as she headed off. "You do know that, right?"

I did my best to stay calm and appear relaxed. Shirley soon returned holding an old ledger book and handed it to him.

"Will there be anything else, Your Majesty?" she said, winking at me.

"No, that will be all for now," he said, staring down at the book as he leafed through the pages.

Shirley shook her head affectionately at the old man and returned to the kitchen.

"If I performed the ceremony, it would definitely be in here," he said, struggling to make sense of what he was looking at. Then he shook his head and handed the book to me. "Why don't you take a look? You at least have some idea of what you're looking for."

I accepted the well-worn book with yellowed pages. I flipped to the first page and glanced at the initial entry.

"1964?" I said. "That was a long time ago."

"It was," he said, smiling. "I do remember that one because it was my first ceremony. I think I was more nervous than the couple getting married. I'd only been here about a month."

"That's amazing." I slowly scanned each page then flipped to the next. "There aren't a lot of entries, especially from way back then," I said, glancing up at him.

"It's a very small island," he said, shrugging. "And tourist weddings didn't really start to get popular until sometime in the Nineties." Then he frowned. "I think it was around that time."

I flipped to another page, and the dates moved into the Seventies. I found three ceremonies conducted on Owen Island in that decade and jotted them down.

"Did you find something?" he said, leaning forward to get a closer look.

"I'm not sure," I said. "I'll have to do some follow-up research when I get back home." I turned the page, moved into the Eighties, and scanned the entries. Then my mouth dropped open, and my neurons started popping. I blinked and set the book down on the table.

"Are you all right, my dear?" Pastor Tim said, studying my shocked expression.

"I'm fine," I whispered.

"I may be old and starting to lose it," he said, chuckling. "But that is the look of a person who just found what she was looking for."

"You're absolutely right, Pastor Tim," I said, beaming at him. "And I couldn't have done it without you. Can I ask you where the owner of the island lives?"

"Bess lives in Atlanta," he said. "Why?"

"I'd like to talk to her."

"Then you're going to need her phone number," he said, glancing toward the kitchen. "Shirley!"

Shirley poked her head into the room, again drying her hands on a dish towel.

"You're bound and determined to make sure I don't get my work done today, aren't you?" she said, this time sounding a bit more serious.

"Oh, hush," he said. "Could you please give our friend Bess Campbell's phone number?"

"That I can do," she said, tossing the towel aside and grabbing a cell phone from the table. She retrieved the number and jotted it down on a slip of paper and handed it to me. "Here you go. You'll need to speak loudly when you talk with her. She's a bit hard of hearing."

"Thanks so much, Shirley," I said, sliding the slip of paper into my shorts. "I can't thank you enough, Pastor Tim." I stood and waited for him to do the same. I extended my hand, and he shook it warmly.

"Thanks for stopping by," he said, studying my face.

"I hope you have a wonderful day," I said, about to turn toward the door but was stopped by the fact he hadn't let go of my hand.

"I'm sure I will," he said, again turning philosophical. "I've been blessed with a very long life, and I've spent it in this beautiful place surrounded by a wonderful family and many, many friends."

A sense of sympathetic dread washed over me as soon as I recognized it was the exact same comment he'd made earlier.

"I guess you really can't ask for much more than that, right?" I said softly as tears began to well in my eyes.

"One can always ask for more," he said. "Like being able to remember what I had for breakfast. But enough about me and my problems. I can't imagine you came all this way to hear my thoughts about the meaning of life or the challenges of old age. How can I help you?"

"Oh, I thought I'd just stop by to say hello, Pastor Tim," I said, blinking back tears. I exhaled loudly and gave him a long, gentle hug. "You take care of yourself."

"I certainly will," he said, now confused. "Shirley?"

Shirley came out of the kitchen and recognized the look on the old man's face immediately. She walked over to him and gently led him back to his chair. He sat down with a smile on his face and looked at me with a curious expression.

"Why don't you get some rest?" she said. "And after dinner, if you're up for it, we'll go for a nice walk on the beach."

"I'd like that," he whispered.

"Don't worry about it," Shirley said, as she turned to me and sensed my concern. "He slips in and out all the time."

"I'm so sorry I upset him," I said, wiping away my tears with the back of my hand.

"No, you didn't do anything," she said, placing a hand on my arm. "Actually, it was probably a good thing for him that you stopped by. I try to make little changes in his daily routine whenever I can. Your visit was perfect for that."

"It's not fair," I said. "He's such a sweet old man."

"He certainly is," she said. "Come, I'll walk you out."

I followed her toward the door but stopped when Pastor Tim called out.

"Thanks for stopping by," he said.

"It was my pleasure, Pastor Tim. It was so nice seeing you."

"It was nice seeing you too…"

"Suzy."

"Of course. Suzy."

I barely made it out the door before the waterworks broke, and I made my way to the Hungry Iguana in the hot late afternoon sun and did my best to navigate the short walk through a veil of tears that momentarily made me forget about the piece of information that, like a hundred dollar bill in the hands of a ten-year old in a toy store, was burning a hole in my pocket.

Old age?

Thanks, but I think I'll pass.

Chapter 24

Gerald and my mother stared at me from across the table like I'd lost my mind. I was okay with that. It certainly wasn't the first time, and I was almost positive it wouldn't be the last. But I was more interested in Josie's reaction. She's much more in tune with how my brain works and has an intuitive feel for when I'm on the right track or about to completely run off the rails. She put her knife and fork down, wiped her mouth, and then nodded at me.

"I think you're onto something," she said. "You don't have it yet, but you're getting close."

"See?" I said, making a face at my mother.

"Darling, I think you're reading way too much into the fact that it might be the same John Smith who got married on Owen Island," my mother said, then glanced at Gerald for support.

"I have to agree with your mother, Suzy," Gerald said, exhaling cigar smoke that got caught in the breeze and drifted across the lawn. "It is a very common name."

"Yes, I'm aware of that, Gerald," I said, agitated at both of them. "But didn't he say that his family originally came from Europe?"

"He did," Gerald said, nodding. "His mother was Czech, and his father was Dutch. But I have no idea what difference that would make."

"The woman's name in the marriage book is Madlenka Bednar. Doesn't that sound European to you?"

"It does," Gerald said, conceding the point. "But what difference does it make? Even if it's the same John Smith, so what? That wedding took place over thirty years ago. Besides, John's been divorced from his wife for years. I don't see where you're going with this, Suzy."

I fell silent. I didn't have a clue where I was going with it, either. But something continued to nag at me, and I was certain there had to be some sort of connection. I pushed my plate away and glanced around for signs of the dogs. All four of them had eventually tired themselves out swimming and chasing each other around the lawn and were now snoozing comfortably next to each other on the cool grass. Earl was in his customary spot in the middle of my mother's lap.

"Bednar is a Czech name," Josie said, glancing up from her phone. "But I'm not getting anything when I search on Madlenka Bednar."

"Have you spoken to the woman who owns the island yet?" my mother said.

"I did," I said, nodding. "It took a while to get through the conversation. She's ninety-nine and almost deaf, but her caretaker was able to help out."

"And she confirmed that someone is definitely trying to buy the island?" my mother said.

"She did," I said, unable to contain my smug grin. "Take a guess who wants to buy it."

"Darling, it's getting late, so let's not play the guessing game, okay?" my mother said, gently stroking the King Charles who was now stretched out across her lap.

"Jansmid," I said, glancing back and forth at them.

Their mouths dropped, and they stared at me, exchanged confused looks with each other, then refocused on me.

"The mysterious company that was referenced in that left-wing rag?" my mother said, frowning.

"That's the one," I said, looking at Gerald. "What do you think?"

"I think it's time we tried a bit harder trying to figure out who this company is," he said, exhaling another cloud of cigar smoke.

"How hard can it be?" my mother said.

"Hard enough," he said. "They aren't registered in Cayman, and if they're doing mostly cash deals, it's going to be hard to trace. And nobody seems to be talking. Which is highly unusual."

"But they'll have to record any ownership transfers with the General Registry office, right?" I said.

"At some point, yes," Gerald said, nodding. "And I'm wondering why they haven't already done that."

"Maybe they're trying to get every deal closed before they let anybody know what they're up to," I said.

"To what possible end?" Gerald said through another cloud of smoke.

"I'm beginning to think that somebody is trying to box you in, Gerald," I said. "Well, not necessarily you, but your government."

"How on earth would they do that?" he said, genuinely perplexed.

"I know you're all under a lot of pressure to do something to appease the conservationists and the environmental folks. They can be really tenacious when they want to be, and I can't imagine you or the Premier is looking forward to all the negative attention they might be able to generate. Not to mention all that bad press. You guys freaked out when *The People's Paradise* published that article. I can't imagine your reaction if it started showing up on the nightly news."

"We have discussed that possibility," Gerald said, nodding. "And we would certainly like to avoid it."

"Suppose this Jansmid outfit was able to buy up a lot of the land you're currently thinking about setting aside for preservation. Or maybe close to the area you're thinking about setting aside as a national park."

"And do what with it?" Gerald said. "Sell all the land to us at an exorbitant price just so we can get some tree huggers off our back?"

"Tree huggers?" my mother said, raising an eyebrow at him. "Really, Gerald?"

"You know what I mean," he said, waving her off. "Our government would never allow itself to be blackmailed like that. And if push came to shove, we could always use our powers of eminent domain."

The wind shifted, and the smoke from his cigar surrounded me.

"That thing is disgusting," I said, waving at the cloud. "You use eminent domain at times?"

"We do," he said, shifting the cigar to his other hand. "But it's certainly not our first choice. Someone always ends up very unhappy when we do."

"But it's used predominantly to provide developers with what they need to build something, right?" I said.

"Pretty much," he said, nodding. "Unless we need the land to build a road or some sort of infrastructure."

"How would the development companies down here react if the government used eminent domain to acquire a lot of land and then watch you set it aside to preserve it from further development?"

"Depending on where the land was located, it might be problematic," he said. "Where are you going with this, Suzy?"

"If someone owned the titles to a lot of the property you wanted to set aside for conservation and agreed to turn it over at a reasonable price, would the government be flexible if the owner wanted to do something different with another piece of property?"

"As I've said many times in the past, pretty much everything is negotiable," Gerald said, shrugging. "Up to a point. Do you have a particular piece of property in mind?"

"Owen Island," I said softly.

Gerald crushed out his cigar then folded his arms in front of him and fell silent, deep in thought.

"No, that would set off a firestorm of protest," he said, shaking his head.

"Not necessarily if it was included as part of a larger initiative like the creation of one or more protected areas scattered around the islands," I said. "You wouldn't be able to bury the news about Owen Island being developed, but it might not get the public reaction it normally would. You could probably spin it as one of the trade-offs you had to make to get the larger deal done."

"I suppose that's possible," he said, scratching his head, bemused. "Still, it's a very small island. What are you thinking, that the CEO of this Jansmid organization is looking to build a personal getaway?"

"I have no idea," I said, shrugging. "But the island is a little over ten acres. It's certainly big enough for that. Or maybe a small, but high-end resort for the uber-rich."

"Perhaps with some sort of eco-tourism theme?" my mother said, glancing around the table.

"That would probably help grease the skids with the government," I said, glancing at Gerald. "What do you think?"

"I must admit that I'm baffled by the whole thing," he said, frowning. "And how is it possible that this Jansmid has been able to stay off the radar?"

"My guess is with lots of cash coupled with the promise of even more if the people selling their properties to them agree to keep their mouths shut," I said.

"Perhaps," Gerald said. "But first we need to figure out who these people are. I guess we could try to look in other locations where corporate identities are protected."

"I could call a few of my friends in Washington to see if they know who this Jansmid is. And if they don't, maybe they'd be willing to do a little research into it," my mother said.

"And I can keep poking around here to see what I can come up with," I said, nodding.

"Or we could just use this," Josie said, staring down at her phone and tapping the keypad.

"What?" I said, staring at her.

"You said this guy John Smith's mother was Czech and his father was Dutch, right?" Josie said, focused on the device in her hand.

"Yes," Gerald said.

"Then I have to say you guys are making this way too hard on yourselves. You're overthinking it."

She held up the phone, and I noticed a language translation app on the screen.

"John in Czech is Jan," she said, glancing around the table. "And Smith in Dutch is Smid. Jansmid. John Smith. Get it?"

We sat in stunned silence glancing around at the table at each other. Then I grabbed the phone out of Josie's hand.

"Let me see that," I said, staring at the screen.

"John is Jansmid?" Gerald said, staring at my mother. "Is that possible?"

"He never stops, does he?" my mother said, shaking her head. "He's always up to something."

"I'm going to need a bit more, Mom," I said, frowning at her.

"John's a what...let's go with wheeler-dealer. But he's certainly not an environmentalist."

Gerald snorted.

"You got that, right," he said. "He once told me the biggest problem with environmentalists was that there wasn't a hunting season for them."

"That's disgusting," I snapped.

"Hey, I was merely repeating what he said," Gerald snapped back. "Don't get your knickers in a knot."

"Well, if anyone would know about the condition of her knickers, it would be Gerald," Josie deadpanned as she reached over and took her phone back.

"Outstanding," my mother said, laughing loudly and giving Josie a golf clap.

"That's what he said," Josie said, grinning and nodding her head in Gerald's direction.

They both roared with laughter.

"Shut it."

I sat quietly for several seconds as my neurons continued to collide with each other. Then an idea popped to the surface.

"Let me borrow your phone for a moment," I said. "Maybe we'll get lucky again."

"Luck had nothing to do with it," Josie said, making a face at me.

I refreshed the translation app and then typed Bednar into the box designated for the Czech entry. Cooper immediately popped up as the English equivalent.

"How about that?" I said. "Madlenka Cooper."

"John's ex-wife changed her name?" Gerald said, leaning forward in his chair.

"We're about to find out," I said, typing the name into the search engine. Seconds later, thousands of search results came back. "Wow. We must be in touch with the universe tonight."

"What is it, darling?"

"Madlenka Cooper. *Doctor* Madlenka Cooper. She's a leading conservationist with two PhDs."

"She's got two doctorates?" Josie said. "Man, that's a lot of school. The woman must be a masochist."

"One's in environmental sciences from Helsinki. The other is in marine biology from a college in North Carolina," I said, reading from the screen.

"We can't be sure she's John's ex-wife," Gerald said.

"Check to see if there are any photos," Josie said, reading over my shoulder.

I clicked on Images, and dozens of photos appeared. I scrolled through several that showed Madlenka Cooper speaking to audiences from behind a podium or in front of a large projection screen.

"Beautiful woman," Josie said, studying the screen.

"Yes, she is," I said.

"Let me see, darling."

I handed her the phone, and she and Gerald spent a few minutes studying the photos.

"Did either of you ever meet his wife?" I said.

"No, he was already divorced before I ever met him," my mother said.

"I knew him when he was married," Gerald said. "But I never got a chance to meet her. I don't have a clue if that's her or not."

I took the phone back and resumed scrolling through the photos. Then Josie grabbed my forearm.

"Hold it," she said, pointing at one of the photos. "Click on that one."

I did, and the photo now filled the screen. It was a picture of the woman in a group shot. She had her arm draped over the shoulder of a young girl whom I guessed was around sixteen at the time.

"Can you read the caption?" I said to Josie, squinting hard. "Either I need glasses, or they're using smaller fonts these days."

"Let's see," Josie said, taking the phone and holding it near a candle that was flickering on the table. "Noted environmentalist, Madlenka Cooper, accompanied by her daughter, Matkazeme, spoke today to the International Society of- ow, watch it, that hurt."

"Sorry about that," I said, after snatching the phone out of her hand. I studied the photo closely, paying particularly close attention to the young girl. "Take a really good look at it."

Josie leaned forward, then flinched and shook her head at me.

"No way," she said. "I can't believe it."

"What is it?" my mother said.

"The girl in the photo, her daughter, is the woman Captain pulled out of the water on Christmas Day."

"Let me see that," my mother said, reaching for the phone. "That is her. I can't believe it. What do you think? Was she down here stalking her father?"

"Either that or she was helping him," I said.

"But why would she disappear into thin air?" Gerald said.

"That seems to be the recurring question," I said.

"Matkazeme?" Josie said. "That's an odd name."

"Let me see the phone, Mom," I said. "Let's give this translation app another shot, shall we?"

I typed the girl's name into the box designated for Czech words, then frowned when I saw the English equivalent.

"Did anything come back?" my mother said.

"Yeah, it did. This is too weird."

"What's the English translation?"

"Mother Earth."

Chapter 25

Like most of the others, New Year's Eve had started off full of promise but ended with a whimper. To be more accurate, it ended with the three of us and the dogs stretched out on recliners at the edge of the pool sound asleep and snoring into a gentle onshore breeze just after eleven o'clock. We'd eaten a wonderful dinner at the restaurant, waited until Chef Claire had finished helping Finn out in the kitchen, then excused ourselves around ten just as the hats and noisemakers were being passed out. We headed home determined to stay awake at least until the stroke of midnight. One glass of champagne later, after we had watched the dogs take a late-night swim in the pool, shared the day's highlights with each other, and discussed the grand opening of the animal shelter scheduled for noon tomorrow the recliners had simply looked too comfortable to pass up.

I've never quite understood the whole *make it to midnight* thing. It's not like it still won't be the new year when you wake-up the next morning. And don't get me wrong; I enjoy a party as much as the next person. But New Year's Eve, for me, has always seemed like a forced, almost mandatory, ritual dictating that everyone with a calendar and a clock have a good time. I much prefer to be surprised and delighted by unexpected revelry instead of bored and disappointed with over-hyped and rigidly timed get-togethers where I'm forced to wear a silly hat and fend off the advances of drunk strangers who consider the stroke of midnight license to lock lips and let their hands roam. And as far as the need for noisemakers goes, I've already got Josie and the dogs to handle that.

I'd come to the realization that I was no fan of the pseudo-festive New Year's Eve several years ago. At first, I chastised myself for being what my mother called an anti-social fuddy-duddy. Then Josie, another outspoken critic of the forced-fun society, suggested that I merely needed to start looking at the issue differently. And since I love to get a good night's sleep, I eventually decided that being fresh and reinvigorated when the calendar turned was an important step in getting the year off to a good start.

Now, being well-rested on the morning of January 1st permanently occupies the top spot on my annual list of New Year's resolutions.

And it's always nice to be able to cross one off the list right out of the gate.

For the record, spending more time at the gym did make its way onto my list of resolutions. But it's way down at the bottom at number thirty-one, and since I'm going to be pretty busy with the top thirty, I'm not sure I'll be able to get to it before Thanksgiving.

I left Josie and Chef Claire still sound asleep on their recliners and headed inside to the kitchen. My first priority was to get a huge pot of coffee brewing. Then I gave all four dogs their morning snack, laid out way too many strips of bacon on a tray and slid it into the oven, then beat several eggs in a bowl. I added a healthy splash of cream, salt and pepper along with a touch of fresh nutmeg, and a handful of cheddar cheese. I poured the mixture into a pan then began cutting thick slices of the Italian bread we served at the restaurant.

The dogs quickly finished their snack and sat in a semi-circle around the oven as the smell of bacon began to fill the kitchen. I ushered them toward the door.

"Why don't you guys go wake those two up?" I said, holding the door open for them. "Maybe go for a swim?"

Chloe cocked her head at me, and Captain dropped a tennis ball at my feet. I grabbed the ball, along with three others, and fired them across the patio into the pool. I watched them charge off and dive into the water then slid the screen door shut and went back to the kitchen. As I closely monitored the progress of the bacon and scrambled eggs, I turned my neurons loose and waited for them to coalesce around this morning's top-of-mind concerns.

High on the list was the need to get some clarification about what the heck John Smith was up to. Gerald had made it perfectly clear that it was also a top priority for him as well. While he didn't come right out and say it, I was certain Gerald was concerned that someone he'd done business with and considered a friend was about to put him in a very difficult position.

Another concern of mine was the genuine fear that something bad had happened to his daughter, the bizarrely-named Matkazeme. Even though it was clear that the woman was a committed environmentalist and probably very much at odds with her father, I couldn't believe Smith had been part of any plan to harm his daughter. As such, I considered it a very real possibility that he wasn't even aware that she had been on Grand Cayman and written the infamous article.

But the fact that she had disappeared without a trace continued to nag at me.

I grudgingly conceded the point that after writing the article she had considered her work done and left the islands to head to the next target in her crusade to slow down what she considered the inexorable onslaught of concrete and condos making their way across the planet. But that would have entailed leaving her beloved Earl behind. Perhaps her next destination prevented her from bringing the King Charles along, but no dog lover would ever leave without making sure their four-legged companion would be well-cared for. And there was no way she could have known that Earl was safe and sound with my mother. That fact alone convinced me that Matkazeme was either dead or being held somewhere against her will.

I removed and drained the bacon then slid it back into the oven to keep it warm. I finished cooking the eggs, removed them from the heat, and focused on the toast. When I had built a buttered stack, I headed for the door and saw Chef Claire and Josie on their feet watching the dogs splashing around in the pool. I waved for them to come inside then set out plates and utensils.

"Good morning," Josie said, coming through the screen door. "Happy New Year."

"Right back atcha," I said. "Hungry?"

"A little early in the day for rhetorical questions, wouldn't you say?" she said, grinning at me as she grabbed a plate.

"Morning," Chef Claire said, picking at her soaked tee shirt. "Where do those guys get all that energy in the morning?"

"Probably from me," I deadpanned as I handed her a plate.

"Good one," Josie said, rolling her eyes at me. "We should try to get to the shelter by eleven just in case Teresa needs any help."

"Sure, that works," I said, sitting down on one of the stools surrounding the kitchen island.

"Good eggs," Chef Claire said through a mouthful. "Nutmeg, right?"

"Yeah, you taught us well," I said. "What time do you need to be at the restaurant?"

Chef Claire laughed and munched a strip of bacon.

"I don't think I *need* to be there at all," she said, shaking her head. "Finn has the place humming. He's amazing."

"Well, he was the executive chef at a major resort down here before my mother convinced him to join us," I said, stacking some of my scrambled eggs on a piece of toast.

"I think we might want to make some adjustments to the ownership structure," Chef Claire said. "I'd like to give him a piece of the action and lock him up so he doesn't go anywhere."

"I was thinking we might want to do the same thing with Rocco," Josie said. "Between the two of them, we wouldn't have to worry about the restaurant at all. I'll take peace of mind over a bit more money any day."

"Okay, that works for me," I said, shrugging. "We pretty much opened the place just so you wouldn't get bored while we're down here all winter."

"I think I'm getting used to it," Chef Claire said, laughing. "This lifestyle gives me a lot more time to sit back and think about what I want to do next."

I looked over at Josie who frowned back at me. Every time Chef Claire started talking about doing something else, we both got nervous that she might decide to leave.

"Oh, relax," she said, shaking her head when she caught the look on our faces. "I'm not going anywhere. Where on earth could I do any better than being with you two?"

"It must be a day for rhetorical questions," Josie deadpanned. "So, what's been on your mind?"

"Two things primarily," Chef Claire said, taking a sip of coffee. "I've been thinking about developing a line of dog food."

"Really? That's interesting," I said, nodding. "Have you gotten anywhere with it yet?"

"Not really," she said, reaching for another piece of toast. "But I think there's a sweet spot we could hit in the market. A lot of the dog food out there is pretty crappy, but there are some really healthy brands as well. The problem is that the dog food that's good for them is so expensive. And a lot of dog owners just can't afford to spend that much money on feeding them. If we can come up with a with a high-quality product and keep the price point down, I think we could do very well."

"Not to mention keeping a lot of dogs healthier in the process," Josie said. "I like it."

"Me too," I said, sliding my plate away. "And it would be a good fit with the dog toy business. That reminds me, the search firm wants us to meet with a CEO candidate."

We'd recently accidentally stumbled into a new business opportunity manufacturing dog toys, and we were currently in the process of getting it off the ground. But our initial CEO had been charged with accessory to murder and was awaiting trial in Ottawa. Given that, we were taking our time and doing our best to make sure we found the right person for the job.

"Who's the candidate?" Josie said.

"She's currently a senior VP with *Cat and Canine Couture*," I said.

"The pet clothing company?" Josie said, frowning. "Oh, I hate that place. Dressing animals up in some of those outfits is just cruel. Captain would probably run away from home if I tried to put him in one of those plaid sweater vests."

"She doesn't like the place either," I said, laughing. "And she's looking for a change and a chance to run a company. The search firm is wondering if we're okay flying her down here for an interview."

"She's a dog lover, right?" Chef Claire said.

"She has two Springer Spaniels that go everywhere with her, including work."

"Okay, that's a very good start. The why don't we get her down here?" Josie said. "We're starting to get a lot of questions about the business we can't answer. I'm completely out of my depth when it comes to things like operational capacity and run rates. What the heck is a run rate anyway?"

"You're asking me?" I said, shrugging. "But I could probably come up with a *leisurely stroll* rate."

They both laughed. Chef Claire topped off all our coffee cups.

"I'll see if we can get something set up for next week," I said. "Well, I must say that this has turned into a very productive morning. The new year is off to a great start."

"Wait a sec. You mentioned you'd been thinking about two things," Josie said, turning to Chef Claire. "What's the other one?"

"Oh, nothing major," Chef Claire said, giving us a coy smile. "I just decided it's about time for me to start thinking about settling down and having a kid. Maybe two."

"And I thought adding learning Spanish to my list of resolutions was a stretch goal," I said, shaking my head. "Wow. You're not messing around this year."

"Thanks to you guys, I've got everything I ever dreamed possible. Except for the family thing," Chef Claire said. "I live in two of the most beautiful spots in the world, we've got the dogs, and with you guys around, my best friends in the whole world, it's like having two of the most special aunties any kid could ever hope for."

"That's so sweet," I said, hugging her.

"Aahhh," Josie said, tearing up. "I'd be honored to spoil your kid rotten."

"I'm serious," Chef Claire said. "I remember I had a ton of extended family around when I was growing up, but my favorite was this woman who used to babysit me. She also helped my mom out around the house taking care of the place. And she would do anything for us. She became such a part of the family that my mom and dad helped her out when she decided she wanted to start her own business. For some reason, you guys remind me of her."

"That's really very kind of you, Chef Claire," Josie said, placing a hand on her forearm. "Isn't it, Suzy? Suzy?"

"Uh-oh," Chef Claire said. "She's got that look."

"Yeah, she's a goner," Josie said, munching on a slice of bacon. "Let's give her a minute."

I eventually refocused on my immediate surroundings. I glanced back and forth at them and blinked several times. I shook my head to clear it and exhaled loudly.

"What is it, Snoopmeister?" Josie said.

"I think I know where Matkazeme is."

Chapter 26

Teresa had done an amazing job getting ready for the grand opening of the shelter. I wasn't exactly sure where all the cats and dogs had come from, but it appeared that we were already nearing capacity. We were also now the official home of a mule, a handful of goats, and a collection of beautiful parrots that were either injured or no longer capable of fending for themselves in the wild.

The outside of the building was adorned with streamers and helium balloons on long strings that were floating high above the ground and being buffeted by a strong breeze. Inside were more streamers and balloons and several dozen people were wandering in and out of the reception area. A lot of them were moving slowly and speaking in hushed voices, victims, I assumed, of their own New Year's Eve revelries. A few of them were still dressed to the nines, their outfits, like themselves, a bit worse for wear. I didn't know most of them and assumed they must have been invited by my mother.

"Well, what do you think?" Teresa said as she approached holding Rocco's hand.

"The place looks great," I said. "Hey, Rocco."

"Hi, Suzy," he said, beaming as he looked around. "Teresa and the kids did a great job, huh?"

"They certainly did," I said. "Who are all these people?"

"I think a lot of them are friends of your mother," Teresa said, glancing around. "A few minutes ago, she told me to get ready for a big day of fundraising. I think she's going to put the bite on all of them for a donation."

"I have no doubt," I said, laughing.

"Excuse me for a sec," Teresa said. "I need to check in with the caterers."

We watched her depart, and the look on Rocco's face was impossible to miss.

"Life is good, huh?" I said, grinning at him.

"Life is amazing. She's amazing," he said. "Are you guys sure you're okay with me moving down here year-round?"

"Absolutely. We need somebody down here to manage the restaurant and keep an eye on things. And we'll find somebody to handle the bar back home."

"I really appreciate everything you guys have done for us."

"The feeling is mutual, Rocco," I said, then noticed Detective Renfro entering reception from the dog area. "What is he doing here?"

"Detective Renfro?" Rocco said, glancing over his shoulder. "My new best buddy? It's like he thinks he's my shadow. Everywhere I go, there he is."

"He still thinks you were the one who shot Gavin?"

"I don't think so," Rocco said, waving at the detective. "But until he has another suspect, I think he feels the need to keep a close eye on me."

"Good afternoon," Detective Renfro said, extending his hand toward me. "And Happy New Year."

"Same to you, Detective," I said, returning the handshake. "Are you thinking about adopting a pet?"

"You know, I wasn't," he said. "But then I saw the most adorable calico cat out there. Given my job and how much my schedule is at the mercy of other people, a dog is out of the question. But a cat just might work."

"Good for you," I said, nodding. "I'm glad I ran into you. Would you have a few minutes to spare? I'd really like to speak with you."

"Sure," he said, nodding.

"I'll take that as my cue to leave," Rocco said, flashing a smile at both of us then walking off to join Teresa.

"He's a good man," Detective Renfro said as he watched him depart.

"He is. Does that mean he's no longer a suspect?" I said, raising an eyebrow at him.

"Maybe," he said with a shrug. "So, what would you like to talk about?"

I glanced around to make sure we were out of earshot of the other guests then gave him a summary of what I believed I'd uncovered. He listened closely as I outlined the details and a few of my conclusions caused him to frown and scowl. When I finished, I couldn't tell if he was giving my theories serious consideration or whether he was simply annoyed.

"What do you think?" I said, rocking back and forth on my heels.

"I think you might be jumping to a few too many conclusions," he said, scratching his head as he stared off into the distance.

"Well, like Josie says, if I didn't, I'd never get any exercise," I said, laughing.

"What?"

"Nothing. Forget it," I said, waving it off. "Where do you think I went off the rails?"

"I'm not sure you did," he said. "But the whole abduction thing sounds like a bit of a stretch. I know her. She's one of the sweetest people on the island. Why on earth would she get involved in something like that?"

"To keep someone she loves safe and out of the way. And to help her former employer out."

"Former employer?" Detective Renfro said. "Where did that come from?"

"That one is sort of a leap of faith," I said, shrugging. "But I'm almost positive I'm right."

"Well, there's only one way to find out," he said. "Let's go check it out."

"Now?"

"If a woman is being held against her will, why on earth would I wait?" he said, suddenly all business.

"Good point," I said, nodding. "Just give me a minute to let a few people know I'm leaving. I'll meet you outside."

I gave Josie and my mother a quick overview of where I was going. As expected, my news generated *have you completely lost your mind* looks from both of them, but they didn't put up much of a fight. I assumed the fact that I was going with a cop reduced their anxiety levels, or they'd simply learned over the years not to waste their breath trying to talk me out of something once I'd made up my mind.

I met Detective Renfro outside, and we decided to take his car since he considered our visit official police business. We made the short drive, and I followed him up the pathway that led to the verandah. I stood directly behind him, and he knocked on the door. Moments later, the door opened and Sylvia, the owner of the guesthouse I'd paid a visit to several days ago, was surprised to see the man standing in front of her.

"Detective Renfro?" Sylvia said, smiling. "It's so nice to see you. And Happy New Year to you and yours. What brings you by?"

If she'd been surprised to see the cop standing on her porch, she was stunned when I took a step to my right and came into view. She flinched, then recovered and forced a smile in my direction.

"Suzy, right?" Sylvia said, brushing her hair back from her face.

"Hi, Sylvia," I said, doing my best to sound casual.

"I have a few questions, and I was wondering if we could come inside," Detective Renfro said.

"Why, of course," she said, taking a step to one side to give us room.

We entered, and I glanced around what appeared to be a sitting area for the guests. Several chairs and couches filled the room, and a large screen TV was mounted on one wall.

"It's quiet," Detective Renfro said, glancing around. "Are all your guests already up and about for the day?"

"No," Sylvia said, unable to maintain eye contact. "Actually, I've recently had some plumbing problems I need to get fixed before I can rent rooms again. Just my luck it happens during one of my busiest times of the year, right?"

She was lying and judging from her reaction to mine, she knew I knew it.

"That is bad luck," Detective Renfro said, sitting down on a couch without being invited.

"You mentioned you had some questions," Sylvia said, still standing, but hovering near the couch.

"Yes. I'm wondering if you've heard from a young woman recently."

"Young woman?" she said, going for coy. "A lot of my guests are women. I meet so many, and they come and go all the time. I'm afraid you'll have to be a bit more specific, Detective."

"Matkazeme Cooper," I said softly. "Is that specific enough for you, Sylvia?"

Sylvia took a step backward as if recoiling from a punch I'd thrown.

"I think she knows who we're talking about," Detective Renfro said as he watched her try to recover.

"Who?" Sylvia managed eventually. "I'm sorry, but I really…" Her voice faded to a whisper then she sat down next to Detective Renfro on the couch. "Yes, she was here at one point."

"Although you weren't willing to tell me her name, you already confirmed she'd been here the time we spoke several days ago, Sylvia," I said, sitting down on the arm of a chair.

"Then why are you here?" she said as tears began to well in her eyes.

"Because we're still looking for her," I said. "The last time I was here, you told me that you used to be a housekeeper for a family on Seven Mile Beach before you opened the guesthouse."

"Yes, I was," she whispered. "What about it?"

"You used to be John Smith's housekeeper, didn't you, Sylvia?"

After listening to my neurons debate how to play it back and forth like an extended tennis rally on the ride over, I'd finally decided to just float the question. If I was wrong, it would save the detective and I some time as well as allow us to get out of the house without being too embarrassed or accused of harassing the woman. But if I was right, and I was almost certain I was, a big piece of the puzzle was about to drop into place. I stared at her with a blank expression and waited.

"Yes," she eventually whispered. She wiped a stream of tears off her cheeks with the dish towel she was holding and exhaled audibly. "But as I told you the other day, she left just before Christmas."

"I remember you saying that," I said, nodding but not taking my eyes off her.

"Can you tell us where she went?" Detective Renfro said. "It would be very helpful. We need to make sure she's safe."

"All she said was that she was going to stay with a friend," Sylvia said, again failing to make eye contact.

"Was that friend a man named Gavin?" Detective Renfro said.

I shook my head even before Sylvia did. Major whiff with that question, Detective Renfro.

"Gavin? A friend?" she said, scowling. "Not likely."

"And since Gavin was also one of your guests at the same time she was, it's not likely she would be leaving here to go stay with him someplace else, right?" I said.

"He was staying here?" Detective Renfro said, frowning at me. "How the heck did you know that?"

"She told me," I said, pointing at Sylvia.

"Don't you think that was something you might have mentioned?" he said, obviously miffed.

"I'm sorry," I said, shrugging. "It just never came up in our conversations."

"A word of advice," he said, glaring at me. "If you expect my help, try not to withhold important facts like that."

"Geez, I said I was sorry. So, you do think it's important?"

"Well, it's definitely something I needed to know," he said, shaking his head. "Amateurs." Then he looked at Sylvia who seemed confused by our banter. "Do you know the name of this friend she was supposed to be staying with?"

"No, I'm sorry. I don't," she said, again failing the eye contact test. But this time she let her eyes drift toward the stairs that led up to the second floor of the guesthouse.

Detective Renfro also caught her subconscious glance at the second floor. He caught my eye and gave me an almost imperceptible nod of his head, his signal that I should go ahead with the idea we had discussed and argued about in the car on the way over.

"Okay, then, I guess we'll be going," Detective Renfro said, placing his hands on his thighs and hoisting himself up off the couch. "Thanks for your time, Sylvia. And we're sorry to show up while you're right in the middle of a construction project."

"What?" she said, squinting at him.

"Your plumbing problem," he said, smiling at her. "I hope it's fixed soon."

"Oh, that. Yes, I'm sure it will be," Sylvia said, getting to her feet. "It was nice seeing both of you. And I wish I could be more help."

"I'm sure you do, Sylvia. But thanks," I said, then immediately transitioned into a frantic, screaming woman. "Earl! How on earth did that happen? Are you okay? Oh, no. Look at all that blood! You poor thing. C'mon, Detective, help me get him to the vet! Hang in there, Earl! Oh, I hope he can survive until we get there!"

Sylvia stared at me open-mouthed like I'd completely lost the plot and glanced around the room for signs of the King Charles.

"What on earth is the matter with you?" she whispered.

Then we heard the soft rattle of chains and a panicked voice coming from the second floor.

"Earl! What's the matter with Earl? Is he okay?"

Then the voice fell silent. Detective Renfro nodded and gave me two thumbs up. Sylvia stared down at the floor.

"I knew it," I said, glancing at the landing at the top of the stairs. "Total dog lover."

"Is there something you'd like to tell us, Sylvia?" Detective Renfro said softly.

She nodded without looking up, then turned and led us up the stairs to the second floor.

Chapter 27

At the top of the stairs, Detective Renfro paused long enough to remove his gun from his holster then nodded at Sylvia to open the door. She glanced down at the gun, then shook her head at the detective.

"You won't need that," she said, opening the door.

"I'm sure you can understand why I might not believe you, Sylvia," he said, racking a shell into the chamber.

Sylvia shrugged then led the way into the bedroom. She moved to one side to give us room, and we saw Matkazeme Cooper sitting on the bed. A long, heavy chain was attached to one leg, and the chain was fastened to a large metal eyelet that had been secured into one of the walls. She glanced back and forth at both of us with a wide-eyed stare.

"What happened to Earl?" she said, panic-stricken.

The woman was bruised and chained to the bed, but her first question was about the well-being of her dog. My respect for her ratcheted up several levels.

"Earl's fine," I said. "He's safe and sound."

"Then what was that I heard?" she said, confused.

"That was a total fake out," Detective Renfro said. "A little misdirection to see if we could get a little cooperation." He glared at Sylvia who was leaning with her back against one of the walls.

"So, he's really okay?" Matkazeme said, relieved.

"He's doing great," I said, smiling. "And certainly a lot better than you."

I took my first close look at her. She had definitely recovered from her near-fatal kayak trip and appeared to be back to normal. That is, apart from the marks all over her face and neck that hadn't been there when we'd found her on the beach. Somebody had definitely given her quite a beating as borne out by the yellow and purple bruises and what appeared to be a broken nose.

"Did you do that to her?" Detective Renfro said to Sylvia.

"Don't be ridiculous," she said, glaring at him. "Of course not."

"Then who did?" he said.

"Gavin," I said softly.

Detective Renfro looked at me then glanced back and forth at the other two women for confirmation. They both nodded.

"Okay," he said, shrugging. "Would one of you mind telling me why?"

They both remained silent. I glanced around the room, didn't see what I was looking for, then turned toward Sylvia.

"Where's the key for that thing?" I said, nodding at the chain.

Sylvia dug into her pocket and tossed me a key that was attached to a rabbit's foot.

"Nice touch," I said, shaking my head at the rabbit's foot. Then I tossed the key to Matkazeme who caught it and unlocked the ankle bracelet. She sighed with relief, then leaned forward on the bed and began massaging her ankle.

"Gavin was furious at you for taking the kayak out on the water, wasn't he?" I said to her. "Were you trying to escape?"

"I'm not sure I'd call it escaping," she said. "But I was certainly getting tired of being told I couldn't go anywhere. Yeah, Gavin was mad. Really mad."

"And when you got discharged from the hospital, he brought you back here, didn't he?"

"He did," she said, continuing to rub her ankle.

"Whose bright idea was it to chain you up?" Detective Renfro said, again glaring at Sylvia.

"It wasn't me," Sylvia said.

"It was Gavin's idea, right?" the detective said, giving them his best stern-cop look.

"No," Sylvia said, shaking her head.

"It was your father's idea, wasn't it, Matkazeme?" I said.

"Yeah," she said softly.

Detective Renfro stared at me in disbelief. I shrugged it off.

"Now that I've got all the junk cleared away, my neurons are finally firing on all cylinders," I said by way of explanation.

"What?" he said, baffled.

"Things are clearing up," I said. "It's like a fog has been lifted."

"Well, then, knock yourself out," Detective Renfro said, making a sweeping arm gesture inviting me to take the lead.

"Thanks, Detective," I said, beaming at him. I looked at the woman who was sitting on the bed with her legs folded under her. "What sort of shape were you in when you were discharged from the hospital?"

"I was a mess," she said, shrugging. "And they'd given me some serious painkillers, so I was pretty much out of it."

"Gavin picked you up at the hospital and brought you back here?"

"Yes."

"That's when he beat you up, right?" I said.

"Was that your father's idea, too?" Detective Renfro said.

"No," I said, jumping in before she could answer. I felt my face flush red with embarrassment. "Sorry, I should let you answer that question."

"That's okay," Matkazeme said, finally managing a small smile. "You're doing pretty good. Please, continue."

"The beating was Gavin's idea," I said. "Somebody wasn't happy that you'd tried to get away, probably your father, and Gavin got chewed out big time for not doing what he was told. And instead of taking it like a man, he decided to take his frustration and anger out on you." I glanced over at Sylvia. "Something he did despite your vigorous protests."

"My protests obviously didn't work," Sylvia said, glancing over at the woman on the bed. "I'm so sorry, Zemmy. Look at what that animal did to her."

"I'll be fine, Sylvia," she said, then glanced back at me. "I slipped out with Earl late on Christmas Eve and headed for the beach. I saw some lights from a boat that was anchored offshore and stole a kayak that was nearby. But the boat was a lot further offshore than I thought."

"That happens a lot," I said, nodding. "It looks like something is only a few hundred yards away in the water, but it can be miles out to sea."

"Yeah, I know that now. And by the time the current and the wind did their thing, I was completely worn out and probably at least a mile from shore. I thought for sure Earl and I weren't going to make it. Then the next thing I remember is being pulled to shore by what I thought was a black bear." She laughed. "Yeah, I must have really been out of it. A bear swimming off Seven Mile Beach, right? At first, I tried to fight it off, but then I realized it was a dog. It was a Newfie that saved our lives, wasn't it?"

"It was."

"I'd like to thank him at some point," she said. "Where's Earl?"

"Perched comfortably on my mother's lap," I said, chuckling.

"His favorite spot in the whole world," she said, laughing. "Can you take me to him? I miss him so much."

"Absolutely," I said, glancing at Detective Renfro who nodded his agreement.

"Thank you," she said, starting to rub her ankle again. "After Gavin beat the crap out of me, he followed my father's demand to chain me up until he agreed it was safe for me to leave."

"Does your father know that he beat you?" I said.

"No, the only people who knew were Sylvia and me," she said, then noticed the look Detective Renfro was now giving Sylvia. "What is it?"

"You were the only one who knew?" he said to Sylvia.

"Yes," Sylvia said, nodding, then caught the inference the detective was making. "Oh, stop it, Detective. I didn't kill that monster. But for the record, I certainly didn't shed any tears when I heard he was dead."

"Do you have an alibi for that night?"

"Yeah, she does," Matkazeme said, nodding. "Me. She spent a couple of hours working on my cuts and bruises. Then we played Gin Rummy the rest of the night."

"Just like the old days, huh?" Sylvia said with a big smile.

"Except you never let me win anymore," Matkazeme said, laughing. "When I was a kid, I used to win all the time. She had me convinced I was a gin rummy genius."

I watched their exchange play out and was soon convinced that the relationship the women shared was long, durable, and steeped in love and mutual respect.

"How long were you the Smith's housekeeper?" I said.

"From the time Zemmy was a baby until she turned twelve," Sylvia said, her eyes dancing with the memories.

"Then my folks split up, and I left with my mom," Matkazeme said. "I haven't been back until a few weeks ago."

"And when that article showed up in The People's Paradise your father knew you'd written it?" I said.

"I'm sure he recognized my writing," she said, nodding. "I've been tormenting him with articles like that for several years."

"And once she showed up at your guesthouse, you had to agree to keep her here because of your relationship with Mr. Smith, right?" I said to Sylvia.

She nodded and plopped down on a chair.

"He said it was essential that I keep her out of the way until he figured a few things out," she said. "And he's always been very good to me. I couldn't refuse."

"And he decided to keep you here just because you wrote that article?" I said, frowning.

"I think that might have been the final straw," Matkazeme said, shrugging. "But like I said, I've been tormenting him for years, and I'm sure he doesn't want me sticking my nose into whatever he's working on down here at the moment."

"You don't know what he's doing?" I said, surprised.

"You read the article," she said. "Did it sound like I knew what he was trying to do?"

"Actually, no, it didn't."

"I know it's Jansmid that's the key to all of this," she said, staring off, deep in thought.

"Oh, it is," I said, nodding.

All three of them stared at me. I glanced around then realized none of them had a clue what I was talking about.

"You don't know who Jansmid is?" I said to Matkazeme.

"No, I don't. Do you?"

"Yeah. It's your father."

"What?" she said, baffled.

"Jansmid is John Smith. It's a play on his name translated into Czech and Dutch."

"That's it?" she said, scowling. "It's that simple?"

"Yeah, I'm afraid it is," I said.

"Then I have to say that I'm more confused than ever," she said, gently touching one of the bruises on her face. "What on earth is he up to? Why all the subterfuge? It's not his style at all."

"His style? I'm not sure I'm following," I said.

"My father is a pretty simple man," she said. "If he can't buy it, build on it, or sleep with it, it doesn't get his attention."

"And in the past, he always just took challenges on headfirst?"

"Yeah, it was sort of his calling card. Maybe the politics of this one are a bit tricky."

"Trying to develop Owen Island isn't going to be easy."

"Tell me about it," she said. "He's in the fight of his life on that one. And that's just me. Wait until I get a dozen lawyers involved and half a million signatures on a petition. I don't get that one. There are dozens of islands in the Caribbean he could buy and build on."

"Maybe he wants it for sentimental reasons," I said, tossing out an idea that had been nagging at me.

"Sentimental? My father?" she said, laughing.

"Well, he and your mom did get married there," I said.

She stared at me then glanced over at Sylvia who was also dumbfounded.

"You didn't know that's where they had the ceremony?" I said, surprised by the news.

"I didn't have a clue," she said. "Sylvia?"

"No, neither one of them ever mentioned it," Sylvia said.

"It was probably a bad memory for both of them," Matkazeme said. "Something they both wanted to forget. Can I go see Earl now?"

"I don't see why not," Detective Renfro said. "But then I'm going to have to bring both of you in for some more questioning. We still have an unsolved murder on our hands, and you two spent a lot of time with the victim."

I drifted off and stared out one of the windows for a long time before turning back to the detective.

"Would it be possible to wait a day on that, Detective Renfro?" I said.

"Excuse me?" he said, frowning at me.

"I think we can wrap this up tomorrow night."

"And just how do you plan on doing that?" he said, folding his arms across his chest.

"Basically by putting all the players in one place and getting them talking," I said.

"Just like that?" he said, shaking his head. "That's all it's going to take?"

"Well, they might need a little help," I said, grinning. "And that's where you and Matkazeme will come in. I'll explain it in the car."

"So, I'll be able to get Earl back tomorrow night?" Matkazeme said.

"Absolutely," I said, then realized how much I was dreading having the conversation with my mother about giving the King Charles back to his rightful owner. "If you can stay here with Sylvia one more day out of sight, I think we'll be able to put all this behind us."

"It would be nice to finally make some sense of all this," Matkazeme said.

"I said we might be able to put it behind us, I'm not sure any of it is ever going to make a lot of sense."

Chapter 28

Detective Renfro dropped me back off at the shelter, but I wouldn't get out of the car until he finally promised to give my somewhat sketchy plan a chance to work. At first, he had resisted and considered my idea incredibly stupid and juvenile without ever actually using those exact words. But when I pushed back and turned snarky, asking him in the most patronizing tone I could come up with if he had a better idea, he acquiesced and agreed to play his part the best he could. He drove out of the parking lot too fast, and his tires kicked dust and sand into the air that drifted and then landed on me. I could have sworn I saw him grinning through the rear-view mirror while I was brushing myself off.

I headed into the shelter and noticed that the crowd had thinned considerably since I'd left. My mother and Teresa were sitting behind the reception desk counting a stack of personal checks, credit card slips, and a pile of cash. I approached, placed my elbows on the counter and leaned forward to get a closer look.

"What did you guys do? Rob a bank?" I said, peering down at the three stacks.

"You wouldn't believe it," Teresa said. "It was like your mom had some sort of power over them. They just kept coming up to me and handing over their money." She stared at my mother, obviously amazing and impressed. "How do you do that?"

"She's an avid collector of compromising photos," I said, laughing.

"Funny, darling," my mother said, jotting the total of the credit card slips on a slip of paper. "It's called knowing how to work a room. Okay, that's the final number." She handed the piece of paper displaying the grand total to Teresa. "That should keep you guys in dog food for a while."

Teresa whistled, then pulled my mother close and gave her a fierce hug.

"I need to show this to Rocco," Teresa said, about to head off, but stopping to give my mother another bone-crushing hug. "Thank you so much."

We watched her head off, then I smiled at my mother.

"You didn't really need to do that, Mom. But thanks."

"Don't mention it, darling. Trust me, they'll never miss the money. And most of them are animal lovers."

"I see," I said, raising an eyebrow. "And the ones that aren't?"

"They're followers who are easily guilted into doing the right thing," she said, laughing.

"You're too much. And my timing isn't very good, but I need to ask you for another favor."

"Okay," she said, sitting back in her chair and giving me her undivided attention. "What do you need?"

"I need you to organize a little dinner party."

"I see. Does this have something to do with John Smith and his daughter?"

"It has everything to do with them," I said. "Oh, and it also deals with who shot Teresa's ex-husband."

"You have been busy, haven't you, darling? I take it you located the woman," she said, draping a leg over her knee.

"I did. And apart from some bruises and the fact that she's been chained to a bed, she's fine," I said, dreading where the conversation was about to go.

"Chained to a bed?" she said, frowning. "Who on earth did that to her?"

"Gavin."

She shook her head, disgusted.

"I'm sure you'll explain everything at some point. When would you like to have this dinner party?"

"Tomorrow night."

"Tomorrow?" she said, nodding. "Okay. It's pretty short notice, but I'm sure we can figure something out. And I assume you have a specific group of people you'd like to invite?"

"I do." I handed her a slip of paper. She studied the list of names then slid it into her pocket. "Will seven o'clock work?"

"Perfect," I said, then grimaced. "Oh, and there's one more thing."

She glanced up at me and waited.

"You'll need to give Earl back tomorrow night."

"Okay," she said, slowly nodding her head. "Of course."

"I'm sorry, Mom."

"No, it's all right. He needs to be reunited with her. And I have two other wonderful dogs that I can't imagine being separated from. She must have been going crazy worrying about Earl."

"She was," I said, trying to read her face. "You're handling this very well, Mom."

"He's not my dog," she said, shrugging. "Can I ask you a question, darling?"

"Sure, Mom."

"What are the chances someone is going to get shot at dinner tomorrow night?"

"Oh, that's highly unlikely," I said, shaking my head. "I'd put it at no higher than five percent." I gave it some more thought. "Ten, twenty percent tops."

Chapter 29

Gerald and my mother listened closely to what I was saying, and then both sat back in unison and folded their arms across their chests. They reached for their Mudslides at the same time, took identical sips, then set their drinks down and placed their elbows on the table as they leaned forward.

"How long did you guys practice that?" I said, grinning back and forth at them.

"It's the universal move for dealing with an insane person," my mother said.

"Tell me about it," Gerald said. "I've heard some bizarre ideas, but you've outdone yourself, Suzy."

"Did you speak with him today?" I said to Gerald.

"I did," he said softly.

"And?"

"And his reaction was what you might expect. He was furious."

"Okay, that's a good start," I said.

"You do know that if you're wrong, it's going to take him a long time to get past this," Gerald said.

"I'm not wrong," I said, hoping my false bravado passed the smell test.

"I just can't believe it," my mother said. "Getting angry about being double-crossed on a deal is one thing. But that's insane."

"Not if you look at it from his perspective," I said, draining the last of my Mudslide. "Can I get you guys another drink?"

"No, I think I need to keep a very clear head," Gerald said. "Just in case the Premier calls me later this evening demanding my resignation and your deportation."

"Don't be so dramatic, Gerald," I said, getting up out of my chair.

I headed for the makeshift bar and poured myself a glass of club soda. Gerald might be acting overly dramatic, but I decided that maintaining a clear head was probably a good idea. Josie and Chef Claire were chatting, and I sat down in the empty recliner between them and stretched out.

"What are you guys talking about?" I said, staring up at the early evening sky.

"We were just trying to come up with ideas for the best way to accessorize a bulletproof vest," Josie deadpanned.

Chef Claire snorted.

"Don't start," I said. "You're worse than Gerald. Nobody is going to get shot. We're just going to have a discussion and let it take its natural course."

"Can we at least eat first?" Josie said. "Dodging crossfire always ruins my appetite."

Chef Claire snorted again.

"Don't encourage her," I said, giving Chef Claire the evil eye. Then I spotted John Smith making his way across the lawn. He waved to us, then sat down at the table with my mother and Gerald. They were soon engrossed in a serious conversation. I noticed Henry leaving the grill area and heading our way.

"Dinner's ready," he said, grabbing a beer from an ice chest.

"What are we having?" Chef Claire said.

"Nothing extravagant," he said, taking a long pull on the beer. "Short notice and all that. We've got chicken, and I picked up some snapper that looked really fresh. We've got a couple of salads, and Chef Claire brought a chocolate cake home from the restaurant. Don't worry, you won't starve."

"You're a good man, Henry," Josie said. "Are you going to be joining us?"

"No, I had a chat with your mother earlier, and she explained the best she could," he said, shaking his head at me. "And I think I might sit this one out. But I'll be around just in case things head south."

"Nothing is going to happen," I snapped. "I wish you people would let it go."

"Let it go?" Josie said, grinning. "Look who's talking."

"Just relax. Okay?" I said, getting up off the recliner. "Let's go sit down and enjoy our dinner."

I led the way as the three of us walked across the lawn and sat down at the dinner table set for nine. My mother, trailed by

Gerald and John Smith, approached the table from a different direction and took their seats.

"Good evening, ladies," John Smith said to the three of us, then glanced around at the other place settings. "We seem to be missing a few people." He unfolded his napkin and draped it across his lap.

"I'm sure they'll be here," my mother said.

Henry approached carrying two trays. He set them down, headed off, then returned shortly with the bowls containing the salads. He asked if we needed anything else, then excused himself. I watched him head for the guesthouse carrying his dinner. I spooned some salad onto my plate, selected a couple pieces of chicken, and began picking at my dinner. I glanced up and noticed John Smith staring across the table at me. I waited it out.

"Gerald said there was something you wanted to discuss with me?" he said, using his hands to work on a piece of chicken. He took a bite, chewed it slowly, the quizzical expression never leaving his face.

"There is, Mr. Smith," I said.

"Please, call me John. Certainly, you know me well enough by now for us to be on a first-name basis," he said, smiling.

"I'm not sure I do, John," I said, waving away the tray of snapper Josie was trying to pass me.

"That sounds rather ominous," John Smith said, digging into his green salad.

"Not really," I said. "I'm just curious about when you had your revelation."

"Revelation?" he said, laughing. "Can I get an amen? Funny, but you don't strike me as an overly religious woman, Suzy."

"Yeah, I'm pretty much church-challenged these days," I said. "But a recent conversation I had has made quite an impact on me. It got me thinking about making amends before it's too late."

"Really?" he said, slicing a tomato wedge in half and popping it into his mouth. "And who do you feel you need to make amends with?"

"Oh, I'm sure there's a bunch of people on my list," I said, laughing. "But I'm not talking about me. I'm referring to you, John."

"I see," he said, putting his knife and fork down and wiping his mouth. Then he sat back in his chair and stared at me. "Who did you have this conversation with?"

"Pastor Tim."

"Pastor Tim?" he said, frowning. "Why does that name sound familiar?"

"Probably because he was the person who performed your marriage ceremony," I said, casually as I reached for my water.

He flinched, then cocked his head at me.

"My marriage ceremony?"

"Yes, on Owen Island."

"You've been busy," he said, reaching for a chicken thigh. He picked it apart and began eating the pieces one at a time. "As the saying goes, what does the fact that I got married on Owen Island have to do with the price of fish?"

"By itself, not much," I said, shrugging. "But when you combine it with some of the other things that are going on at the moment, it's an important piece of the puzzle."

"So, now you're trying to solve a puzzle?" he said, glancing over at my mother. "You certainly have raised a most inquisitive daughter."

My mother gave him a small smile and raised her glass of champagne to me in salute. But she remained silent as she took a sip then set her glass down on the table.

"Please, continue, Suzy," John Smith said, draping a leg over his knee. "I can't wait to hear where this is going."

"I guess my curiosity really started getting the better of me when I read the article your daughter wrote for *The People's Paradise*."

"My daughter?" he said, immediately dropping his leg and sliding his chair closer. He placed his elbows on the table and leaned forward. "How on earth did you know she's my daughter?"

"Well, it wasn't easy," I said, exhaling loudly. "But we eventually put it together. Josie helped a lot."

"Feel free to leave me out of it," Josie said, gently sliding another piece of fish onto her plate.

"We found a picture of her standing next to your ex-wife," I said. "We recognized her as the same woman we rescued on the beach."

"I see," he said, nodding. "Well, I have to say that it's nice to be able to finally thank all of you for saving her life. I'm eternally grateful."

"Josie's Newfie is the one you need to thank," I said.

"Where are your dogs? I don't see them anywhere," John Smith said, glancing around the lawn.

"We left them home tonight."

"Then we must be headed for a very serious conversation," he said, chuckling. "I imagine it takes a lot for you to leave your dogs behind."

"It does," I said. "And that was another major driving force behind my…inquisitiveness. I just couldn't accept the fact that your daughter would leave without taking her dog with her. Or at least checking to make sure he was okay before she left."

"I'm sure she had her reasons," he said, reaching for another piece of chicken. "Matkazeme rarely does anything without a good reason."

"Unless she wasn't able to make her own choice, right?" I said, glancing at him over the top of my water glass.

"I'm not sure if I should be offended by your obtrusiveness or congratulate you," he said. "But I am impressed. I wouldn't worry too much about her. I'm sure she's safe and sound."

"She is," I said, nodding. "But at first, I wasn't sure. And when I spoke to your ex-wife she told me that Matkazeme hadn't checked in with her for several days. She was quite concerned."

"You spoke with Madlenka?" he said, giving me a wide-eyed stare.

"I did. She seems like a very nice woman. And incredibly bright."

"She's the smartest woman I've ever known," he said, momentarily glancing off into the distance. "What else did she have to say?"

"Just that you were really sick," I whispered.

"Yes, I am," he said eventually with a small shrug. "But she shouldn't have told you that."

"Why didn't you say something, John?" my mother said.

"What's the point? The last thing I want is a bunch of well-wishers hovering over me and watching me disintegrate before their eyes."

"Still, you should have said something," Gerald said.

"Well, now you know," he said, picking up his fork and getting back to work on his salad.

"Your ex-wife also said that you told her to get ready for a major surprise," I said.

"Yes, I did," he said, perking up. "And it's going to be a wonderful surprise." Then his eyes narrowed, and he glared at me. "Unless you've got it figured out and plan on ruining it."

"I don't want to ruin anything," I said softly. "But I do think I've got most of it figured out."

"I see. And how many people have you shared it with?" he said, now on the defensive.

"Just Gerald and my mom. And I think Gerald has told one person. Isn't that right, Gerald?"

Gerald nodded and fiddled with the unlit cigar he was holding.

"You told Oliver, didn't you?" John Smith said.

"Yes," Gerald said softly.

"Oh, that's not good," John Smith said. "I was planning on telling him at my last doctor's appointment, but I couldn't bring myself to do it."

"He's not very happy," Gerald said.

"I'm sure he isn't," John Smith said. "I'm about to cost him several million dollars. You invited him to dinner, didn't you?"

"Yes," my mother said. "He's coming over as soon as he finishes up at the hospital."

John Smith grunted and shook his head. Then he rubbed his head with both hands.

"Double-crossing Dr. Couch probably wasn't the nicest thing you could have done to someone who helped you get your daughter out of the hospital," I said, toying with the food on my plate.

"The decision was made long before the situation with my daughter occurred. They're not directly related."

"She never should have been released from the hospital that quickly. She almost died on that beach."

"She was very well cared for," he said. "Oliver made sure of that."

"And Sylvia," I whispered, then peeked up from my plate to gauge his reaction.

Shock was the closest term I could come up with.

"Your reputation is well-deserved."

"Thank you," I said. "And I can say for a fact that Matkazeme is doing fine."

"You've seen her?" he said, stunned. "How did you figure out where she was?"

"That one was driving me crazy," I said, shaking my head. "But as soon as I came up with the idea that Sylvia used to be your housekeeper, it made perfect sense. And now that Matkazeme is gone, I'm glad that Sylvia will be able to get back to her normal life."

"What are you talking about? My daughter has left Sylvia's house?"

"She has," I said, nodding.

"And you know this how?"

"Because she's in the kitchen," I said, casually gesturing toward the house.

Moments later, Matkazeme came out of the house with Detective Renfro walking by her side, and Earl cradled in her arms. She slowly approached the table, sat down next to my mother, and glanced nervously around the table. Eventually, her eyes landed on her father and stayed there.

"Hi, Dad," she whispered.

"What on earth happened to your face?" he said, gently reaching out to examine her bruises.

She flinched and sat back out of reach. She made room for the King Charles on her lap and took a gulp of water.

"Your hired thug, Gavin, did it," she said. "As punishment for trying to get away and making him look bad in the process."

"Then he's a very lucky man he's dead."

Josie frowned and glanced up from her plate. She raised a finger and was about to speak when she caught my head shake.

"Let it go," I whispered across the table.

She shrugged and went back to work on her dinner.

"I hope you know I had nothing to do with that, Zemmy," John Smith said, still mesmerized by the bruises on his daughter's face.

"I know," she said, stroking the dog's head. "You were just responsible for my abduction, right?"

"Just to keep you out of the way until this deal was done," he said, his eyes pleading with her.

"What is it this time, dad? A thousand condos with a golf course and views overlooking the parking lot? Or maybe some more of those monstrosities designed for a family of twenty instead of the two people that usually end up living in them?"

"No, this is a very different deal," he said, with a sad shake of his head. "And I was hoping you wouldn't hear about it until after I was gone."

"Gone?" she said, frowning. "Where are you going next, Dad? I hear there are some prime locations in Central America ripe for the taking."

"Matkazeme," I whispered with a soft shake of my head. "Don't."

"Don't what?" she said, scowling at me.

I stared at John Smith who eventually took his cue.

"I'm sick, Zemmy," he said. "Really sick."

Matkazeme's eyes grew wide, then she began tearing up. She placed a hand on her father's arm, and he gently patted her hand.

"Why didn't you tell me?" she said.

"Because there's nothing anybody can do," he said, exhaling loudly. "But I was going to tell you soon."

"Does Mom know?"

"She does. I told her a couple of weeks ago."

"And you thought that instead of telling your own daughter, kidnapping me would be the perfect parting gift?"

"As soon as I read that article, I knew you were around. And I have to admit that I panicked when I realized it. I had to get you out of the way in a safe place. Sylvia was the perfect choice. I'm about to surprise several people, and some of them are going to be very upset with me. I couldn't take the chance that they might try to get back at me by harming you."

"What on earth could you be doing that is going to upset that bunch of crooks? No offense, sir," Matkazeme said, giving the Finance Minister a quick glance. "You've probably made all of them a gazillion dollars by now."

John Smith fell silent, then he looked across the table at me. Our eyes locked, and a big grin slowly formed on his face. He sat back in his chair, chuffed.

"Okay, you're on, Suzy," he said, beaming at me. "You think you've got it all figured out, dazzle me with your brilliance."

"Geez, John," Josie said, shaking her head. "Don't encourage her."

Everyone at the table laughed, with the exception of Matkazeme who continued to stare blankly at her father. More than happy to accept his challenge, I sat back in my chair and organized my thoughts.

"I think it's all wrapped up in your desire to make amends, John," I said, starting slowly. "With your daughter and your ex-wife. Both of them have considered you…well, for lack of a better term, a parasite laying waste to everything that crosses your path."

"Really? Parasite?" Josie said, shaking her head. "Geez, Suzy, don't sugarcoat it. Why don't you tell us what you really think?"

"And the only thing I can come up with that might possibly change the way they feel about you and what you do for a living is for you to do something neither one of them would believe you're capable of."

"I can't wait to hear this," John Smith said.

"Me either," Matkazeme said, leaning forward in her chair.

Earl grumbled his displeasure when his available real estate got cut in half, and she picked the dog up and gently handed him to my mother. Earl stretched out on my mother's lap but kept a close eye on what was going on at the table.

"Along with making amends, I think you're also dealing with some questions about what sort of legacy you'll be leaving behind. All that money is nice, but just having your name on a bunch of condo complexes probably isn't all that appealing." I paused to take a sip of water. "How am I doing so far?"

"Keep going," John Smith said.

"So, to make amends with your ex-wife and daughter, both committed conservationists, and to leave a lasting mark on society, I'm pretty sure that your plan is to hand over a whole bunch of land to the government with the proviso that it be set aside as protected. I'm guessing your new foundation is going to focus on the preservation of marine life."

"My new foundation?" John Smith said. "How on earth do you know about that?"

"I've been keeping an eye on new records coming into the General Registry," Gerald said. "That one came through a couple of days ago."

"Well, technically it's registered as a Jansmid entity, but we all know that's you," I said, slowly chewing a bite of chicken.

John Smith flinched again, seemed confused momentarily, then shook it off and gestured for me to continue.

"And your use of Jansmid was what made it so hard to figure out what the heck was going on. And it also made Matkazeme's article very hard to follow."

"Yes, it did," he said, smiling.

"You've been buying up a ton of land," I said.

"I'm always buying land," he said, shrugging.

"You've been telling your investors that you're working on a major development deal, haven't you?"

"It is a major development deal," he said. "It's just not the sort that investor group is used to seeing. But there will be some buildings and infrastructure that need to be built."

"You're setting up some sort of marine research facility down here, aren't you, John?" I said, smiling across the table at him.

"Yes, I am. I am thoroughly impressed, Suzy." He grinned at me, then turned and beamed at his daughter. "The Cayman Mother Earth Institute. Dedicated to the study and preservation of the natural habitat here and around the Caribbean."

"What?" Matkazeme said, staring in disbelief at her father.

"And my hope is that your mother will agree to run it," he said.

"But you're still planning on buying and developing Owen Island," Gerald said, frowning. "John, I don't have to tell you how big a public relations nightmare that would be."

"Develop it? Absolutely not," he said, shaking his head. "But I have bought it."

"To what end?" Gerald said.

"To make sure it stays untouched," he said. "When we got married there, Madlenka said that people could wonder all they wanted if paradise could actually be found on earth, but that little islet was proof of its existence. Owen Island will be one of the centerpieces of the Institute." He stared off into the distance. "I can already see your mother walking the beach or diving in the coral. She's going to love it."

"Who's going to love what?"

All of us turned in our seats and saw Dr. Oliver Couch standing a few feet away. None of us had heard him arrive, and he had definitely caught us by surprise. I studied his face closely, and, as I expected, he was glaring at John Smith.

"Hello, Oliver," John Smith said.

"Have a seat, Oliver," my mother said, gesturing at the remaining place setting. "I hope you're hungry. We have a ton of food."

"Thanks, maybe I'll eat later," he said, glancing briefly at my mother before sitting down and fixating on Smith. "How could you do that to me, John? We go way back."

John Smith exhaled, then shrugged his shoulders at his friend.

"I'm sorry, Oliver," he said. "But I needed that piece of property. And you refused to sell it to me."

"I was going to build on it," Dr. Couch snapped. "Two dozen luxury condos. Each one with an oceanfront view. Do you have any idea how much I would have made on that deal?"

"A little over sixteen million," Smith said, shrugging. "But that land parcel is sitting right in the middle of where the Blue Iguana sanctuary is going to be located."

"If you had mentioned what your plans were, I'm sure we could have come to an agreement," Dr. Couch said.

"I couldn't say anything to anybody, Oliver," Smith said softly. "Word would have gotten out, and the prices people would have wanted for their land would have gone through the roof."

"So, you decided to run a scam on the people you've worked with all these years?"

"Technically, it's not a scam, Oliver," Smith said, trying to downplay it. "Everyone, including you got more than fair market value for your land. You're just not going to make what you expected to. But remember, Oliver, you did eventually make the choice to sell it."

"Only because you sent that henchman posing as a Jansmid representative to my house threatening to break my legs," Oliver snapped, his face beginning to flush red.

"Gavin wasn't posing," Smith said, shaking his head. "He was a Jansmid employee. In fact, he was the only employee. And I apologize for his behavior. I did not give him instructions to threaten or hurt you. But as it turned out, he was a little hard to control."

John Smith nodded at his daughter, then reached out to gently stroke the side of her bruised face. Matkazeme flinched at first, then let him continue without protest. Dr. Couch glanced at the woman and seemed to see her for the first time.

"Zemmy?" he said with a scowl that morphed into a forced smile then became a puzzled expression that remained on his face. "It's so nice to see you here."

"No thanks to you, right, Dr. Couch?" she said through narrowed eyes.

"I'm sorry," he said, backpedaling. "But that was your father's idea. He wanted you out of the hospital and taken someplace safe."

"So I've been informed," Matkazeme said, glancing back and forth at him and her father.

"You played me," Dr. Couch snapped, refocusing his anger on Smith.

"Yes, I did," Smith said, staring back at him. "But you more than got your initial investment back. And it's for a good cause.

Actually, I'm thinking about naming one of the Institute's buildings after you."

Dr. Oliver Couch's face had officially turned crimson, and he gripped the table with both hands and began taking deep breaths.

"I'm going to sue you and Jansmid for everything you've got," Dr. Couch whispered.

"You're too late, Oliver," Smith said softly. "I've already transferred everything into the Institute. And the rest of my personal funds have been bequeathed to Zemmy and Madlenka."

"What?" Dr. Couch said, wincing in his chair.

He glanced at Gerald who confirmed the news with a nod of his head.

"All the paperwork came through in one big batch to General Registry today," Gerald said.

"My lawyer has the new will. And Jansmid no longer exists as a corporation," John Smith said.

"How is that possible?" Dr. Couch said, slamming a fist on the table. The sound reverberated across the lawn, and Earl flinched and tucked himself under my mother's arm. "How did you pull that off?"

"Everything was handled in cash," Smith said. "The people I was working with on this deal operate on a cash basis. They needed their money laundered, and I made that happen. It cost me a small fortune to make it work, and they're not going to make what they thought they were going to, but I made sure they were taken care of. The last thing I would want is for Zemmy or Madlenka having to worry about those people after I'm gone."

"Organized crime?" Matkazeme said to her father.

"Close enough," he said, patting her hand. "But you won't have to worry about them. I've given my lawyer a long list of names and a detailed description of their operations." He paused and glanced at Gerald. "Just so you know, Gerald, your name's on the list, too."

"What?" Gerald said, almost coming out of his chair. "I don't have anything to do with those people, and you know it."

"Yes, perhaps," John Smith said with a coy smile. "But if they ever raise their ugly little heads down here, she's been instructed to make sure the government and the media get copies of everything." He stared off toward the beach and shook his head. "Getting involved with those people was the worst thing I ever did. Except for letting your mother get away, of course."

"Did that animal Gavin work for them?" Matkazeme said, subconsciously touching her face.

"Yes, he did," Smith said. "I think they were looking for somewhere to put him and get him out of their hair. From what I hear, he was a major source of embarrassment to their outfit. I'm so sorry I turned him loose on you, Zemmy. You too, Oliver."

"He got what was coming to him," Dr. Couch said, wincing and pressing a hand against his shoulder.

"Yes, he did, didn't he?" John Smith said, grinning at Dr. Couch.

"Here we go," I whispered to Josie. "Buckle up."

"What?" Josie said, glancing down the table.

"You'll see," I whispered, then gave Detective Renfro a quick wave. He gave me the briefest of nods and remained focused on the interplay between Dr. Couch and Smith.

Dr. Oliver Couch stared across the table at the smile John Smith was giving him and frowned.

"What are you grinning at?"

"I'm just happy that Gavin got what he deserved," John Smith said. "And I guess I have you to thank for that, Oliver."

My mother and Gerald sat upright in their chairs. I leaned forward to keep a close eye on Dr. Couch's hands that were once again gripping the table edge.

"Why would you thank me?" Dr. Couch whispered.

"For shooting that despicable cretin, what else?" John Smith said, shrugging.

Dr. Couch's eyes grew wide. Stunned, he looked around the table with an expression like he'd been hit in the head with a hammer. My mother and Gerald both sadly shook their heads in silence. Josie and Chef Claire exchanged surprised looks, then both of them focused on me.

"Dr. Couch killed Gavin?" Josie whispered.

"Yeah," I whispered back.

"How the heck did you figure that out?"

"Shhh," I said, holding a finger to my lips.

"I shot Gavin? Nice try, John, but I think your illness is starting to affect your thinking," Dr. Couch said, doing his best to laugh it off but failing miserably.

"I must say that I was delighted the night he got shot," John Smith said. "And that was before I even knew what he'd done to my little girl." He looked down the table at me. "Did you also have this figured out?"

"Yes," I said, nodding. "I wasn't sure for quite a while, but after talking with Detective Renfro yesterday, I was convinced Dr. Couch did it." I flashed a sad grimace at the doctor. "I'm so sorry, Dr. Couch."

"Well done. That's very impressive," John Smith said, glancing back and forth between the detective and me. "It was the caliber of the bullet, right?"

Detective Renfro and I both nodded.

"I was quite surprised when the ballistics report finally came back," Detective Renfro said.

"I was completely wrong about the size of the gun used," I said. "I was positive it was a twenty-two. You know, nice and light and quiet. Just a couple of soft pops in the night air."

"But it wasn't a twenty-two, was it?" John Smith said, glancing across the table at Dr. Couch.

"No, it was a twenty-*five* caliber," Detective Renfro said. "Close, but very different."

"Especially in popularity," I said. "Twenty-twos are all over the place. But according to Detective Renfro, you don't see many of twenty-five caliber pistols down here." I looked at Dr. Couch. "And it's the sort of gun that a collector might have. Like someone with an interest in antiques."

"And our registration system confirmed that you own a twenty-five-caliber pistol, Dr. Couch," Detective Renfro said. "We'll need you to turn the gun over so we can do some testing."

"I gave him that pistol for Christmas several years ago," John Smith said. "Remember, Oliver?" He looked around and spoke to the table. "It's a beautiful antique Colt. And you do love your antiques, don't you? I remember the day we took it to the firing range. I was quite impressed with both the gun and your ability to shoot with it."

Dr. Couch sat quietly, but his breathing was labored.

"And you left the restaurant right after Rocco had not so gently removed Gavin from the premises," I said. "If I remember correctly, you said you needed to get back to the hospital."

"I did have to get back," Dr. Couch whispered. "One of my patients had developed an infection."

"But it would have only taken you a minute to two to locate Gavin's car behind the restaurant and take him out," I said. "And as long as you did go to the hospital, nobody would have given it a second thought."

"Except for the gun," John Smith said. "That was a big mistake, Oliver."

"It was the only gun I had," he finally said, beaten, staring down at the grass between his feet. Eventually, he looked up and pleaded to Detective Renfro. "He came to my house earlier that day demanding that I sell my land to Jansmid. If I didn't agree, he threatened to hurt my son." Then he glared at John Smith. "This is all your fault."

"A lot of it is, Oliver," he said, nodding. "But I didn't shoot him. If it's any consolation, if it were up to me, I'd give you a medal."

"You're disgusting," Matkazeme snapped at her father. She got to her feet, lifted Earl off my mother's lap, and headed inside the house.

John Smith watched his daughter depart, then spoke to my mother.

"Do you think I should go after her?"

"No, John, I don't," she said. "Just give her some time to sort some things out. Like answering the question of whether or not she wants to acknowledge you as her father."

"I was only trying to make sure she was safe," he protested. "And set her and her mother up in something they'll both love."

"I'm not questioning your motives, John," my mother said softly. "Only your methods. And, by the way, your methods suck. Sending that animal to threaten Oliver? Abducting your own daughter? And putting her under his control? You should be ashamed of yourself."

John Smith sunk lower in his chair and seemed to become smaller from the full-on assault of my mother's fury. I felt a tinge of sympathy for him. I knew exactly how he felt.

Been there, done that.

I caught my mother's eye and smiled at her.

"You're going to pay for this, John," Dr. Couch said, climbing to his feet.

"Please sit down, Dr. Couch," Detective Renfro said, immediately transitioning into full-on cop mode.

"Don't tell me what to do," Dr. Couch said, raising his arm and pointing a finger at John Smith. "You and I are by no means finished with this, do you understand?"

John Smith sat quietly at the table, apparently preoccupied with thoughts of his daughter.

"I said, do you under..." he said, his body stiffening as his eyes grew wide. "Do you-"

He reached into his pants pocket, and Detective Renfro jumped to his feet and pulled his gun.

"No, wait," I said, scrambling out of my seat and positioning myself between Dr. Couch and the detective who was already pointing his gun at the doctor.

"Suzy, you need to move. Now," Detective Renfro said, racking a shell into the chamber.

Then Dr. Couch slumped forward and fell face first onto the table.

"It's his heart," I snapped. "Put your gun away. He was reaching for these." I bent down and picked up the bottle of pills he'd dropped on the ground. I fumbled with it but finally got the childproof cap off. "Call for an ambulance, Mom. How many do you need?"

"Three," he whispered through a groan.

I placed three of the pills in his mouth and then held a glass of water to his lips. He managed to swallow the pills, then Josie and I helped him stretch out on the cool, damp grass. His breathing pattern was irregular, and his face was ashen.

"He's having trouble breathing," my mother said. "He shouldn't be on his back. Help him sit up."

Chef Claire grabbed some cushions off the recliners, and we used them to support his back. Josie and I held his shoulders, and my mother draped a couple of beach towels over him. We continued to hover around him as we waited for the ambulance.

"I think I'm going to be okay," Dr. Couch eventually managed to get out. "Thank you."

"Just sit there and take it easy," I said.

"I can't believe it," he whispered.

"Can't believe what, Dr. Couch?"

"That I'm a murderer."

"I had some trouble believing it, too," I said, gently squeezing his shoulder.

"Can I tell you something?"

"Sure."

He wiggled a finger for me to come closer. I leaned over, and he whispered in my ear.

"Can you keep a secret?"

"I'll do my best," I said, frowning. "But I should probably tell you that my track record isn't great."

"I'm supposed to do everything I can to preserve life and do no harm."

"Sure, sure. The Hippocratic oath and all that, right?"

"Yes," he said, lowering his voice even more.

"What do you need to tell me, Dr. Couch?"

"Shooting that despicable creature felt great," he whispered into my ear.

I caught the look in his eyes and the tight grimace I'd seen on the faces of evil people before.

It caught me completely off guard, and I recoiled.

Perhaps Dr. Couch merely wanted to get it off his chest to make room for the thousand-pound weight that was currently constricting his breathing.

Perhaps that look wasn't the sole province of the truly evil.

Perhaps it lurked somewhere deep in all of us and was capable of rising to the surface during extraordinary circumstances.

I forced my neurons to move on, to focus on something else.

But I kept my promise to him and didn't tell a soul.

Epilogue

Dr. Couch spent a week in the same hospital he'd spent most of his career working in and fully recovered. At least as fully recovered as a man with a failing heart could hope to achieve. He remained under armed guard the entire time, and the news of his arrest for the murder of Teresa's ex-husband spread faster than my incident in Gerald's office. But since he knew everyone on the island, and was on a first-name basis with every cop, lawyer, and judge, he wasn't considered a threat and was granted bail. He's officially retired from practicing medicine and spends all his time relaxing at home and doing everything he can to make amends with his son while awaiting trial. Or until his heart gives out.

Probably not the way he'd anticipated spending his golden years.

Frederick moved in with his father and turned *The People's Paradise* over to Jessie, the woman who had helped me place our original ad in the paper. The ads have been very successful, and we continue to advertise with her on a regular basis. One of the first things she did after taking charge was to get rid of all the 'workers' along with the posters that had been hanging on the walls. And she also painted the place and replaced the carpet. Now, the paper's articles are more focused on the *paradise* themes people normally associate with Caribbean vacations. Instead of *up the workers*; the primary thrust of most articles is *down the food and drink*.

I'm pretty sure that Karl would have hated the changes, but Groucho would have loved them.

Madlenka Cooper arrived a few days after her daughter and ex-husband had reconnected at my mother's house. Her loathing for the man she bore a child with was evident, and her reaction to the bruises on Matkazeme's face was predictable. John Smith continues his efforts to make amends with both of them, and while the creation of the Mother Earth Institute is a big step in the right direction, the clock is ticking faster, and I'm not sure he's going to make it before his time is up.

But the mother and daughter seem committed to making the Institute work, and Gerald has pledged the government's support in making it happen. He was given the unenviable task of making sure the community of real estate developers can live with the thought that at least some of the mangrove swamps might escape the onslaught of bulldozers and cement trucks. Gerald has certainly got his work cut out for him, but I heard through my mother that he is already working with a group of investors on an eco-tourism resort to be built near the Institute.

His new mantra, *'there's no reason the environment and a growing economy can't co-exist,'* seems to be catching on and I hear that *The People's Paradise* is planning to do a three-part interview with him.

And the wheels on the bus go round and round.

Now that things have quieted down, we've finally been able to settle into a daily routine that works for the three of us and the dogs. We usually get up early and take the dogs for a walk on the beach before the sun begins to bake everything in its path. Then we'll check-in with home to make sure everything is going well at the Inn as well as make jokes about the weather down here compared with the snow and mind-numbing cold Sammy and Jill are dealing with. For some reason, they don't find the jokes quite as funny as we do. After that, we'll either hang around the pool with the dogs or take a day trip. A visit to the shelter is usually followed by dinner, either at the restaurant or back at our place or my mom's with friends and their dogs. Then we'll usually settle in for a movie and a snack or a late-night swim. It's certainly not an exciting lifestyle, once you exclude the murders, but we wouldn't change a thing.

Except eliminate the murders.

We're getting pretty tired of dealing with them.

My mom has adjusted quite well to the fact that she is no longer responsible for taking care of Earl. But Matkazeme makes it a point to stop by often with the dog who frequently manages to run into a lawn chair or trip over a garden hose. We'd originally thought his clumsiness was the result of the bump on the head and eye injury he'd gotten during the ill-fated kayak trip. But according to Matkazeme, who shakes her head in disbelief every time the little guy stumbles or trips over something, Earl is actually, in fact, a bit of a klutz. Which only adds to his cuteness factor.

And don't tell my mother, but we're already scouting around for King Charles puppies and plan on giving her one for her birthday.

But today we've decided to finally pay a visit to Owen Island. Matkazeme and her mother have made it very clear that they have no intention of making any changes and that anyone who wants to spend some time on the island is more than welcome. So I find myself enjoying the stiff breeze as Captain Jack's boat effortlessly cuts through the water as we head for Little Cayman. All four dogs are sitting in the shade with their heads up and their tongues lolling as they enjoy the breeze.

I'm finally back in a two-piece suit, but one that provides ample coverage of all areas that remain white and untouched by the sun. Josie and Chef Claire are sprawled out, and, like me, slathered in sunscreen, sunglasses on, hats pulled down low. We're not speaking at the moment because they believe I've changed my mind about visiting the island since I've refused to succumb to their demand that I join them on a kayak trip from Little Cayman to Owen Island. I have every intention of joining them on the island, but they don't know that yet.

Captain Jack slowed the boat as we approached the dock, and I hopped out to handle the lines. Josie and Chef Claire made one last attempt to convince me to join them, but I politely refused, and they headed for the kayak rental place in a mild huff. Captain Jack watched them go, then looked at me.

"They seem upset with you," he said, laughing.

"They'll get over it," I said, reaching down to pet all four dogs that surrounded my legs.

"I'm not sure they know what they're getting into. They're going to be fighting that headwind the whole time. It's a short trip over there, but it's gonna take them a lot longer than they think."

"Yeah, I know," I said with a big grin. "I guess we'll just meet you at the Hungry Iguana later."

"Take your time," he said, nodding.

"Conch fritters and Mudslides, right?"

"You're a quick study," he said, leaning forward to give the dogs one final pet before heading down the dock.

I followed him halfway down the dock, then stopped and climbed into a flat-bottomed boat equipped with a small outboard engine. As he had promised, Pastor Roy had left the keys inside a cooler filled with sandwiches, snacks, and several large bottles of water. I reached into my bag then tossed a fresh bag of bite-sized Snickers into the cooler. I poured one of the bottles of water into a portable dog dish I'd brought along, then a second, and waited until the dogs had drunk their fill. I glanced out at the water and saw two yellow kayaks being buffeted by the wind. I grinned, then whistled for the dogs to get into the boat, and I untied the lines. The engine started on its first pull, and I slowly headed away from the dock for the short trip to Owen Island.

A few minutes later, the dogs started barking like crazy when they recognized who we were following. Josie and Chef Claire turned around then stopped paddling. Immediately, the wind started blowing their kayaks back toward Little Cayman. I slowed the boat as I approached.

"Having fun?" I said, grinning back and forth at them.

"You little cheater," Josie said, resuming her paddling. "You lied to us."

"I didn't lie," I said, shaking my head. "I just said I wasn't getting in a kayak. I didn't say anything about not taking advantage of the remarkable advancements in technology. Like the outboard motor. Geez, it's really windy today, isn't it?"

"Maybe a little," Josie said, shrugging.

"I'd offer you a ride, but the two of you seem pretty satisfied with your choice to paddle," I deadpanned.

Chef Claire wiped the sweat off her brow with the back of her hand and glared at me.

"You had this planned the whole time?" she said.

"I did," I said, grinning at her. "One phone call to Pastor Roy to get the weather report was all I needed. Geez, that looks like quite a workout. I would have joined you, but working up a sweat like that is way down on my list of New Year's resolutions. So, I guess the dogs and I will just meet you over

281

there. I hope there are still some sandwiches left when you finally get there."

"You got sandwiches?" Josie said.

"I do. Along with some snacks and a case of cold water," I said, waving one of the bottles in the air. "Oh, and a fresh bag of bite-sized on ice. Just the way you like them. Not frozen, but really chewy."

"I'm gonna kill you, Suzy," Josie said, pointing her paddle at me.

"You'll have to catch me first," I said, placing my hand on the throttle. "Wanna race?"

I opened the throttle, and the boat slowly surged through the water. Eventually, the sound of their protests faded, and I chortled with a big, goofy grin on my face as I watched the pristine stretch of sand come into clear view.

Still laughing, I glanced down at the dogs.

"Can you believe the mouths on those two?"